TIGHT WOMEN
IN
HARD PLACES

By Alicia Night Orchid

TIGHT WOMEN IN HARD PLACES
Alicia Night Orchid (author)
Published by Logical-Lust, copyright 2010

ISBN: 978-1905091-75-1
Paperback version
Published by Logical-Lust Publications © 2010

Cover image by Helen E. H. Madden, pixelarcana.com
© Logical-Lust Publications 2010

Tight Women in Hard Places is a collection of works of fiction. The names, characters, and incidents are entirely the work of the author's imagination. Any resemblance to actual persons, living or dead, or events, is entirely coincidental.

DEDICATION

This book is dedicated to Ray and Mary.
You know who you are.

CONTENTS

Preface by Cole Riley 9

The Anatomy of Wet 13

Smoke 19

Royal Orleans 26

I Saw the Light 40

Fridays Without 53

Third Shift 72

Ray's Opening 95

Savage Nights 115

A Lover in the House of Spies 129

Snowbound 138

Voyeur Nation 158

The Western Front 170

Torn in Two 185

About the Author 209

Other titles by Logical-Lust 210

ALICIA NIGHT ORCHID'S
TIGHT WOMEN IN HARD PLACES:
AN APPRECIATION PREFACE BY COLE RILEY

"Living never wore one out so much as the effort not to live."
                                    - Anais Nin

Yes, there is so much to say about this book. Alicia Night Orchid's stunning collection of thirteen stories contains the spark of life, and it will speak for itself with each new reader, with each new mind open to its many secrets. Like any work of art worth its salt, its fictional alchemy restores sensual sanity in this modern plasticized world, bringing a heightened sense of love and lust from a feminine consciousness that can only enrich our jaded selves with its eroticized tales of resilience, empowerment, and fulfillment.

So Alicia Night Orchid's fictional world is fresh and new. It's new because its men and women talk and behave like real human beings do. They are not afraid to live or to love. They act in ways like real people do when they are blindsided by the heated chemistry of sexuality and sensuality. She writes simply and boldly of women feeling unsure about themselves, feeling nervy about men, feeling uneasy about the soft flesh they inhabit, feeling frantic about the urges and desires which make pleasure a priority.

This is not smut. This is not porn. This is about revelations and discoveries of the human kind. This is about real people in real situations that involve the often confusing, turbulent themes of love and lust. Alicia Night Orchid gets inside the heads and bodies of her people. She paints lines of economic beauty and sizzle when she talks of bodies seeking comfort and bliss. Not one of her stories contain a boring series of cookie-cutter sex scenes which often fill other countless books.

Take her first story, "The Anatomy of Wet," where she depicts two college kids entranced with the miracle of young love, which is fleeting as a fickle downpour. In her tale, "Smoke," she chronicles the parade of bad boys and one-nighters of a wealthy, powerful woman who needs to go "slumming" before she returns to that alabaster address on Pennsylvania Avenue. The story has a surprise ending worthy of O. Henry. Witness her memorable fable, "Royal Orleans," where she re-creates the moment of emotional seduction in the mind of a young woman eager to know love:

> **"And yes...yes, you're sure you made the right decision, because his kiss is like falling into a well that you never wish to leave. You kiss him back—tongues swirl, nipples harden, and suddenly you're floating, floating, and you've said yes, you want to see him again."**

In two other Alicia Night Orchid stories, "I Saw the Light" and "Fridays Without," it is the small details that form their narrative glue; all strung together like the bittersweet lyrics of a Cajun blues. The former yarn features a honky tonk gal who loves a good time but somehow has lost her bearings in this mix of the spiritual, the secular and the sensual. The latter story has a special place for technology running amok, taking Kate the bespeckled librarian into some forbidden realms of desire.

Conflict, crisis, resolution. This is life itself. Toss all labels, classifications, and categories out when you read her stories. The characters of Tammy the hustle gal, Ray the aeronautic engineer and his "shyster bitch" are as real as can be in the next couple of stories, "Third Shift" and "Ray's Opening." The fate of the hapless Ray in the last tale is a somber life lesson with his girlfriend making him her bitch and he loves it. Outlaw Amour 101.

The stories, "Savage Nights," "Snowbound," and "Voyeur Nation" all engage the mind, jolt the soul and fire up the libido. Somehow the woman reminds one of the Jimmy Stewart role in Hitchcock's *Rear Window* as "peeping Pauline" in "Voyeur Nation," watching a couple perform while knowing they're on display. But the other tales, "A Lover in the House of Spies," "Torn In Two," and "The Western Front" display a versatility and high craftsmanship rarely found in this genre.

There will always be a public debate about the merits of erotica versus porn. This is high-style erotica told with style and flair. It is similar to the well-penned imaginative work of Anais Nin, D. H. Lawrence, and Henry Miller. This is the good stuff. Read it, feel it, and be moved.

Cole Riley

THE ANATOMY OF WET

Rain streaked the window. Wind rattled the bare trees. Low-hanging clouds skittered across the morning sky—steel gray, always the same. We hadn't seen the sun in weeks.

"It doesn't rain like this in California."

He wouldn't say, but I knew what he was thinking. No one was forcing me to stay.

"You're not listening. This fucking rain is driving me crazy."

We'd been together since UCLA. After graduating, I could have gone for a PhD at Berkley. Instead, I followed him to Indiana.

"At least it's not snowing," he said.

"I hate this rain."

His head was in that book again. "Labia majora. Labia majora."

Didn't anyone appreciate the difference between active and passive voice anymore? Was the art of the opening line so hard to grasp?

He dog-eared his page. "Don't you have a class to teach?"

"How about papers to grade?"

"You could study."

He frowned at me. "Well, I've got an anatomy exam tomorrow. I have to study."

"Make us some coffee. How about some bacon and eggs?"

I wheeled on him. "Make your own goddamn coffee."

I slammed the bedroom door, threw myself onto the bed, and pulled a comforter over my head.

Two seconds later, he was there. "Hey, Em, what's wrong?"

"Leave me alone."

"Emily, talk to me."

"Why should I? You never talk to me. Worse yet, you don't listen. You haven't heard a word I've said in months."

He turned on a bedside lamp and sat next to me. "Here. You should see this."

"What is it?"

"It's pretty cool. Look."

I crawled out from under the comforter and propped up pillows. Open on the bed between us was the large, heavy book he'd been studying. Drawings of disembodied female genitalia stared up at me. Arrows connected text to body parts.

"You think that's cool?"

"It's more complicated than the male anatomy."

"Anything's more complicated than the male anatomy."

"Anyway, here's what I was trying to memorize earlier. Mons pubis. Did you know that's what it's called?"

"Sure, I guess."

He placed his palm flat against my mons. "I love the way yours stands out so prominently in your swimsuit."

I rolled my eyes. "You're full of shit."

"No, really. Especially that black one-piece. It's so sexy."

"Are you trying to make me feel better?"

"Sure, why not?"

"So, what else you got?"

"These are the labia majora." His index finger sketched a circle between my legs. "It means large lips."

"I know what it means. I was an honors student, too, remember?"

He pushed my panties aside. "See, here's the mons and there are the labia. This is your pubic hair."

"Pubicus harrius," I said with a wink.

He combed through the curly blonde patch, then scratched his nose. "I love your scent. Always have. It's earthy and sweet at the same time."

I punched him in the chest. "Like I said, you are so full of shit."

He gave me a sly grin. "These here are the labia minora."

A fingertip traced the line of my slit.

"Sure enough."

Two fingers opened me. "Wow, there's the outer urethra. Just like in the book."

"My pee hole."

"Yeah, and let's see, here's the vaginal opening."

"Uh-huh."

"You seem to be missing a hymen."

"You should know." I'd surrendered my virginity to Hayden my sophomore year in a dorm room bed.

He wriggled a finger inside. "Nice and tight. Kinda moist."

I leaned back, resting against the pillows, my pelvis thrust forward. "That's what I hear."

He probed deeper, curled his finger, and applied pressure. "I think this is referred to as the G-spot."

I gasped. "That's definitely the spot."

"And there's the cervix."

"Yep." I squirmed, unable to sit still.

He withdrew and tugged at my panties. "Maybe we should take these off."

I lifted my hips. "How's that?"

He lowered his face between my thighs. "Now this particular region is referred to as the prepuce of the clitoris."

"The hood."

"Yes, the hood."

I felt his tongue, warm and slippery.

"Tastes good too."

"Just like honey. That's what all the boys say."

"Really?"

"Well, just one."

He smiled up at me with shining eyes. "This is the glans of the clitoris."

His tongue darted and swirled. I squealed like a little girl.

"Sensitive, isn't it?" Hayden feigned seriousness. "My book says the clitoris has the second most nerve endings of any part of the body."

"What has the most?"

"We'll get there."

His lips closed around my clit and he began to suck.

I placed a hand on the back of his head. "That's really good."

He licked me like a kid with an ice cream cone.

"Yeah, baby, just like that."

Now, two fingers played in and out. I humped his face.

Just when I was finding my rhythm, he paused. He held his hand up for me to see. A gossamer string of nectar stretched from his fingertips to my opening.

"Amazing lubrication," he said.

"It happens," I managed.

"Should I . . ."

"Definitely."

I bit my lower lip as he returned to his business. The squishy sounds of my pussy drowned out the falling rain.

"That's really good," I encouraged him. "Yeah, right there. Just like that."

"Lift your legs."

"Okay."

His tongue searched lower. "Let's see. This is your perineum."

I giggled. "Ooooh. That tickles."

"I can stop."

"No, don't stop."

"Here's that really sensitive spot. The anus, they call it." He barely grazed it.

"Oh my."

He wet his thumb with saliva. He massaged my rectum while licking and sucking my clit. "How's that?"

"That works."

"I could eat you forever."

"Oh, baby. Oh, my God."

I gave in to him. His tongue, his thumb. His tongue, his thumb.

I rocked and bucked. Lightning flickered in the distance. Thunder rolled across the prairie. I came like a flood.

"That's my girl, that's my girl," he murmured. His eyes locked on mine over the soft rise of my mons.

"Oh, Hayden." I pulled his body over mine, my breasts flat against his chest.

He kissed me, then nuzzled into the nape of my neck. "This'll pass, Em," he whispered. "It won't be like this forever."

His erection throbbed on my belly. "I know. I know."

"We'll get through this."

"I know."

"I love you, Em."

"I love you too, Hayden. Now, fuck me. Fill me up."

He slipped his cock out of his boxers and pushed inside. My face turned to the window.

"Look," I said.

But he was in the moment, the slap and the thrust, his breath a cacophony in my ear.

Outside, the rain had stopped. The sky had brightened.

It wasn't exactly sunny, but it was clearing.

SMOKE

She found this one in the Mark Russell Lounge of the Omni Shoreham. Kennedy had held his Inaugural Ball here. Clinton, too, that old horndog. It was a nice, old, dignified place, a tidy distance from the White House.

Mark Russell, the placard said, was a musician who'd come to play piano for a two-week stand. He'd been so popular and well-liked he stayed for twenty years and had the lounge named in his honor following his death.

But she wasn't looking for Mark Russell's ghost.

The man in her sights was at the opposite end of the bar—alone, nursing a drink, and smoking.

She ordered a glass of Chardonnay from the handsome young waiter and watched the man in the bar's mirror. Her nipples stiffened when he drew on the filtered end of his cigarette, held the smoke momentarily between his parted lips, then allowed it to drift outward only to suck it back in like a whip lashing a bared ass.

In seconds, he expelled the smoke in a thin stream. It coiled above him, a dark and threatening cloud.

She crossed her legs and bit her lower lip. Her panties were already damp. She felt flushed and hot and dreamy with it, her hands sweaty and icy at the same time.

The man was neither young, nor good-looking. His hair was thinning at the crown and his eyes were burdened beneath by folds of flesh. He was shorter and pudgier than her husband, but he smoked beautifully.

She waggled a finger at the bartender and nodded toward the end of the bar. He poured another glass of wine for her, another drink for the gentleman, and moved her tab. She slid off the barstool and sauntered across the lounge. Even though she was on the other side of forty, the line of her long, lean legs and the roll of her firm buttocks moving beneath sheer fabric were enough to catch more than one man's attention.

Maybe one of them recognized her, or thought he did, but she doubted it. She wore her hair shorter than it appeared in photos or on TV, almost as short as a boy's. She wore glasses, a tasteful black dress that stopped just short of her bare knees, and five-inch Manolo Blahnik heels.

She reserved a more demure appearance for the cameras.

The man gave her a surprised smile when she sat next to him and introduced herself as Emily Carter. He thanked her for the drink and fished another cigarette from his pocket. She was quick to light it for him.

He was a Bob, or Jim, or Bill. Never an Andrew, Pierre, or Ethan.

She asked where he was from.

Iowa, or Nebraska, or Bumblefuck. Never McLean, or Alexandria, or The District.

She said she was there on business.

He said he was leaving tomorrow.

There was always this small talk to get past.

Her father, a powerful and wealthy man, had smoked. She remembered watching him from the backseat of his leathery

Cadillac, her pubescent thighs pressing together, anticipating something she was too young to even imagine.

Her first boy had smoked, although smoking was forbidden at the Baptist church camp where he served as counselor. Bobby McCord was a preacher's son, tall and lean, the baddest, sneakiest of all the preachers' sons she'd known over the years. He'd held his cigarette in the corner of his mouth the entire time, not even losing it when she redeemed him, white and sticky, in the palm of her hand. She wiped it on her skirt before skipping off to prayer service.

When it came time to date, the young men her parents and teachers approved of were clean-cut. Often, they were athletes or academics or the Goody-goody Two-shoes type—church ushers and the like. They didn't drink, smoke, or swear. They asked permission before kissing her goodnight.

Then she discovered another kind of young man in the crosstown bars she sneaked off to—first, in high school, then later, in college.

These were young men with long hair and dirty nails. Young men who worked the line, swilled beer, and fought in the parking lot. They squeezed her tits when she brushed past on the dance floor, grabbed her ass while she waited in line for beer, and pushed her knees apart in the backseat of muscle cars with the top down on hot Texas nights.

And after she fucked them, rode and spurred them like a cowboy on a bucking steed, they'd lay back on the Naugahyde and light up. With her head resting on their substantial chests, she'd indulge herself in the smoke leaking from their churlish lips.

When they could, she'd fuck them again, slick and hot, legs splayed across their corded bellies, until she cried out. She'd look down at them and watch the smoke gathering about their beautiful faces like a wreath.

Yes, yes, fucking yes.

Before they married, her husband had a reputation as a party boy. But, God bless him, he gave it up—the cigars, the scotch, the partying—for her and Jesus. He was the perfect choice for a woman of her status, but not her needs. Back home, she had no problem finding discreet, accommodating men who understood, even appreciated, a woman like her. Here in Washington, under the media glare and given security considerations, it required more than discretion and accommodation to achieve a smoky tryst.

Those first few years, she lived on memories and fantasy. More recently, she'd found a way—strangers in hotel bars, men on the move in town for only a night or two.

Men who smoked.

She told him to meet her in the men's room—Bob, or Jim, or Bill, or whatever the fuck his name was.

He was reluctant, but she assured him it would be worth it.

He grinned and shook his head. "You're not some kind of freak, are you?"

"I'm a little freaky. It's not necessarily a bad thing."

"We're adults. We could go upstairs to my room."

She stood, flipped a fifty onto the bar, and pushed her barstool in. "Meet me in the bathroom first. And bring your cigarettes."

She sat on the toilet and positioned him in front of her. She looked into his eyes and told him to light up. He licked his lips.

"Okay," he said, a little breathy now.

"Nice and slow," she told him while stroking his cock through his trousers.

He gave a flicker of a smile. "You like that? The smoke?"

She watched it trickle from between his lips, watched him draw it back in a flash. She pressed her thighs together, just like in Daddy's car.

"What do you think? Yeah, I like it."

She unzipped his pants, reached inside, and took his cock in her hand. She drizzled saliva over it, her eyes never leaving his. He dragged deeply, exhaling smoke through flared nostrils.

"Fuck, woman."

He hardened and she took him into her mouth. They were always primed, these men, overworked and deprived of sex at home. That's why she did this here, first—to take the edge off, but also to test them. To determine if they understood and were willing to comply before taking them upstairs and fucking them hard and true.

She peered up at him, tongue flicking, one hand stroking, the other inside her dress pinching a nipple.

"Suck it," he whispered, spewing smoke.

The cigarette dangled at the corner of his mouth. She bobbed and jacked, nursing him between her soft, red lips. Suddenly, his hips bucked and he grunted. She withdrew and his semen squirted onto the bathroom floor and wall.

"Shit. Goddamn," he said. "Motherfucker."

She stood, took the cigarette from him, and inhaled deeply. He took the hint and kissed her, accepting the smoke as it passed between them. His hands slid down the back of her dress and cupped her ass.

She nibbled his ear. "You up for this, Jim Bob?"

"I think so."

She dropped the butt onto the floor and ground it out with the toe of her shoe.

"Come on," she said. "I'm in 308."

She sat on his chest, her knees pinning his shoulders to the bed. Her pussy oozed nectar bare inches from his face.

"That's it," she directed him in the near darkness, "just like that."

He dragged on the cigarette, then licked her slit and suckled her clit, the smoke engulfing her cunt. She reached low and rubbed herself while he blew deep inside her, the sweet man.

When he was hard, she squatted over him, fit the condom, then lowered herself. Their eyes locked and he French-inhaled. She milked her nipples with her hands as she bounced and moaned.

He lasted and lasted and lasted, smoking and looking up at her through the trails and wisps. It hit hard and fast, like a storm off the Gulf. She spasmed, belly clenching, thighs shuddering. As a courtesy, she allowed him to finish pumping and thrusting while she lay atop him.

Before she left, they shared a final smoke, standing naked, side by side, at the window. Snowflakes showed in the lights of passing cars.

He knew enough not to ask questions.

The young man from behind the bar awaited her at the elevator. He'd abandoned his bartender's attire in favor of the standard-issue dark suit and tie. He nodded, but refused to look her in the eye. A barely noticeable wire escaped his ear and disappeared into his shirt collar.

Downstairs, one of the men who'd eyed her in the lounge held the limousine door open. The beefy fellow she and "Jim" had encountered as they exited the men's room was now behind the wheel.

A middle-aged woman in the familiar dark suit sat across from her, legs crossed primly, a look of disgust playing across her face.

"You smell awful," the woman said.

"Just get me back," she answered.

The driver checked the traffic over his shoulder and pulled onto the snow-slick street. "I'm on my way," he said into his microphone.

When they made the familiar turn onto Pennsylvania Avenue and the large white house surrounded by the wrought-iron fence loomed in front of them, the woman in the dark suit spoke up again. "At least use the employee entrance. You can clean up there."

"Emily" pressed her nose against the window, her breath causing fog to form. "Mind your own damn business."

It really wasn't that difficult. At first, she'd thought they didn't know. After a while, she'd decided they didn't care. She supposed her husband and his cronies had enough on their plate.

The car pulled to a stop.

Life, or something like it, began anew.

ROYAL ORLEANS

Years before Katrina and the devastation it visited on New Orleans, I lived in that beautiful city's embrace for a while. I rode its streetcars late at night and jogged in Audubon Park come morning. I ate its food—raw oysters and red beans and rice and crawfish *etouffee*—and washed it down with an ocean of beer. I sunbathed in its blistering heat and cooled myself in the shade of its great live oaks. I slept naked on damp and wrinkled sheets and awoke to the scent of gardenia and jasmine drifting through my window. I bared my breasts in exchange for Mardi Gras beads and allowed myself to be felt up by strangers on Bourbon Street.

And, for the better part of a semester, I engaged in a blistering affair with one of my professors.

I was a freshman law student at Tulane, anonymous except to a few friends, and struggling to decipher the difference between appellant and appellee, the meaning of *res ipsa loquitur,* and the consequence of *res judicata.* My professor taught Contracts and was self-assured and well-known throughout the legal community. I sat in the front row of his class, my face shining with all the intelligence I could muster, lips parted, brown eyes wide open. For his class, I even managed a little makeup and the occasional skirt, a major change from the usual worn jeans and flannel shirt.

One day, about halfway through the semester, I noticed him watching as I sauntered into the classroom. I noticed him smiling at me before and after class. And I caught him looking at my legs as I sat, knees primly pressed together, ankles interlocked.

He was in his mid-forties. He was well-dressed—dapper, even—in his linen trousers and silk sport coats. He was smart, articulate, and good-looking. And he was manly in a way the young men I'd already been with were not. He was broad-chested and thicker about the middle than I was accustomed to. He wore a goatee, had large, soft hands, and a boyish smile. I was a svelte twenty-three. My legs were strong and lean, my breasts sat up high without the aid of a bra, my stomach was flat and as rippled as a washboard, and my ass, so I was told, was to die for.

I paused after class to ask him a question one day. It was a genuine question about one of the cases we'd been asked to read, not a mere ploy to gain even more of his attention. At least, that's what I told myself. He waited until the other students cleared the room before turning to me. He listened and studied me while I talked. When I was finished, he cocked his head and asked if we could discuss it over a cup of coffee.

You probably know how these things go. One cup of coffee leads to another. Over the first cup of coffee, the professor answers your question. He flatters your intelligence and explores the pros and cons of various arguments. He claims that you are one of his best students and that he appreciates your participation in class.

Over the second cup of coffee, he pauses, places his hands on the table, and looks you in the eye. He confesses that he's attracted to you, even though he's married and has teenage children. He realizes he's older than you and acknowledges that you probably have a boyfriend. He admits that there may not be a future in this, but still, he needs to tell you how he feels. Is there any chance his attraction might be mutual, or has he misread the situation entirely?

And because you're young and unattached and relatively inexperienced. And he's attractive and worldly and there's really no chance of attachment to him. God knows, attachment is the last thing you want, anyway. And maybe because you're flattered that he thinks you're smart enough to keep his company and pretty enough to arouse him. And maybe because he's got power and money and offers to take you places you've only dreamed about going before, you tell him yes. Why, yes, you're attracted to him too.

So, he walks you across campus, along a leafy street lined with old mansions and great live oaks with Spanish moss hanging from their branches. The air is still and warm. When you reach the entrance to the house where you've rented a room for the semester, he glances about to make sure no one is looking, takes your hand, and kisses you. And yes . . . yes, you're sure you made the right decision, because his kiss is like falling into a well that you never wish to leave. You kiss him back—tongues swirl, nipples harden, and suddenly you're floating, floating, and you've said yes, you want to see him again.

A few days later, he took me to Brennan's for brunch. We ate eggs Benedict and drank expensive champagne. Afterwards, he led me by the hand to a grand old hotel that used to be called the Royal Orleans on Rue St. Louis and—at least, before Katrina—was owned and operated by the Omni Hotel chain. It was the middle of a weekday afternoon and, save for a few conventioneers, the place was deserted. He rented a room for the day, as if it were the most natural thing in the world. He kissed me in the elevator and I nipped at his ear. He was dressed in a white linen suit and a bow tie. When I pressed against him, I could feel him harden and his hot breath on my neck. I was in a thin cotton dress with only a white thong underneath. I was sweaty and dewy and damp between my legs. I wanted him, and I really wanted him to want me.

Our suite on the fifth floor overlooked the street. It was well-appointed with a four-poster bed, a fireplace, and a soft, inviting sofa. It was sun-splashed and dappled with shade from the nearby trees and buildings. I rushed in and flung open the French doors that led to our balcony. I stood grasping the wrought iron railing, inhaling the scene beneath me—the people, the horse-drawn carriages, the scents of food and sweat and liquor and lust. He stood behind me, lifted my hair, and kissed me lightly on the nape of my neck. He pressed his pelvis against my rump, and I could feel him hard and thick and long. He reached around and felt my breasts through the thin fabric of my dress, gently at first, then squeezing, then milking, then pulling at the nipples until I thought I'd scream. I laid my head back against his shoulder, swooning, gasping, then kissing and kissing and kissing.

Standing there on the balcony with the people below looking up my dress, he pushed the straps off my shoulders, sucked gently on an earlobe, and bared my full breasts to the world. He laid his soft hands on their nakedness, pressing them together, pinching each nipple between his thumb and forefinger. I reached behind and squeezed him through his trousers and was rewarded with a groan of pleasure.

"I love your breasts," he breathed, and it sounded like an explosion in my ear.

He took my hand and led me back into the room.

"Don't close the doors," I told him. I didn't want to lose touch with the city, the sights and the sounds.

He backed me against the wall next to the bed, held my hands out flat, and kissed my breasts, burying his face between them. His beard chafed; his teeth nibbled. He drew my skirt over my hips and pressed a knee between my thighs. I humped against him like a bitch in heat. His hands slid down my back and cupped a buttock in each.

"Oh, your ass . . ."

I was hot and willing and ready to be fucked. I pushed his jacket off his shoulders, unbuckled his belt, and unzipped him. I reached inside his undershorts and held his cock—his beautiful, slick, hard cock—in my hand. And at the same time, he slipped a hand inside my thong and touched my pussy. He felt me swollen and wet and smooth, because I'd shaved for him just that morning. Then he stepped back and looked me in the eye, smiling.

"You're wet already, aren't you?"

"Yes."

"You want it, don't you?"

"Yes, God yes."

"Tell me what you want."

"I want you to fuck me."

"You want to be fucked hard, don't you?"

"Yes."

"You want me to make you come, don't you?"

I ground my cunt against his hand, trying in vain to draw his fingers inside me. "Yes, yes, and yes."

"Beg for it."

"Please, please."

"Say it."

"Please fuck me, please fuck me hard."

"And . . ."

"Fuck me until I come. Make me come, please . . ."

And then his pants were on the ground along with my thong, and he took me standing up, right there, because we both needed it at that instant. I hooked a leg around his waist and he put both hands under my ass and pushed inside me. I arched my back to meet him and took him deep. I ground my clit against his pelvic bone as he thrust in and out.

He pumped me hard, my ass thumping against the wall. I whimpered like a little girl, singing in rhythm to the slap of his cock and the suck of my cunt. The tension built in both of us like a wire drawn taut between two galaxies, until the wire snapped and I started to come—one of those crazy, indecent times when you start and just keep coming and coming. I was clawing him and humping and crying *yes, yes, yes* when the white-hot pleasure in my pussy got even hotter.

He thrust and grunted and filled me deep, gushing, emptying his pitcher into my vessel and gasping over and over, "You sweet bitch, you sweet bitch, you sweet bitch."

I whispered, breathy in his ear, "Yes, I am. I am your bitch, your sweet, lovely bitch, Lanie."

The professor's name was Jonathan, but he went by Jack, and said that I could call him "J" if I wished. He called me Lanie, "sweetness," or "love." I teased and told him he could call me "L."

He bought me jewelry, flowers, expensive champagne, and fine dinners in the best restaurants. Although I'd been fucked before, and fucked well and truly by college boyfriends and men I'd met on summer jobs, I'd never been worshipped like this. He'd kiss me for hours, tease my nipples to a tremulous tension, then bring me to the brink with his mouth on my pussy.

His lips were soft and warm, probing and sucking, and I loved how he talked to me while he ate me, telling me how beautiful I was, how wonderful I smelled and tasted, how much he loved it when I came on his face.

Then, in the end, when I'd already come once or twice, but needed that final hard release, he'd slide his beautiful cock inside. We'd rock for what seemed like hours on the expensive bed, bathed in the tawdry lights of The Quarter in our suite at the Royal Orleans. After I'd spasmed with him deep inside me, clawing at the sheets and his back, he'd take it out and show it to me. He'd rub it between my breasts, across my lips, on my sensitive and needy clit, until he shot, thick and white, both of us watching and gasping and thrashing about.

On the days we couldn't meet, he'd leave me notes and tell me all the things he wanted to do to me. He'd describe the positions he wanted me in—hands and knees, on my side, riding him, facing away from him so he could watch his cock dip in and out of my sweetness. And, of course, I'd masturbate to his notes and write back to him, describing in detail how he'd driven me to madness in my bed, in the backseat of a deserted streetcar, among the carrels in the law library, standing shamelessly at my window looking out over my gardened street in the early morning, my hand in my panties, working, working, working.

The semester ground on—Torts, Civ Pro, Property Law, Criminal Law, and, of course, J's Contracts. I learned the language of the law—negligence and proximate cause, jurisdiction and venue, life estates and springing interests, criminal intent and double jeopardy, consideration and *quid pro quo.*

One day, J told me he'd been offered a deanship at another university. It was a long shot, but he was going for the interview. It was a logical next step in his career. A week later, I had a short story accepted at a prestigious literary magazine and began to wonder why I ever wanted to be a lawyer.

My story was about a man who lives a double life, dividing his time between two wives, two jobs, and two sets of children until he's forced to choose, only to discover he cannot, because his one life is these two lives. The evening I received word that my story had been accepted, I stood on the sidewalk outside of J's elegant home. I stood in the street like a vagabond and watched him dine with his family.

Afterwards, I took the streetcar to the French Quarter, the smell of electricity all about me, the heavy autumn breeze in my hair. I got off at Canal and Bourbon Streets and walked the three blocks to the Desire Oyster Bar. I ordered a straight shot of Chivas, knocked it back, and then I ordered another.

A tall, angular man sat down beside me. His brown and gold hair was uncombed and he hadn't shaved for several days. The bartender slid a Dixie in the man's direction and accepted a five in return.

I allowed my eyes to run over the man's body. Strong, tanned legs rose out of ancient leather sandals and disappeared into loose-fitting shorts. I would have wagered a hundred dollars that he wasn't wearing underwear. A well-worn Hawaiian shirt clung to his shoulders. He'd left the first few buttons open, revealing a vest of thick, curly hair.

He said his name was Cole. I lied and told him my name was Marianna Marissa Delacroix. We talked and drank. I made up a story about how I was a teacher and was on a sabbatical to see the world. He said he tended bar at a place on Lake Pontchartrain. We drank more, and my lies got bigger— never forget that everything a writer tells you is partly truth and partly fiction. I said I had only a few months to live, having caught a rare and deadly disease in the jungles of New Guinea. He said he'd never met anyone like me.

I rested my hand on his bare knee while looking him straight in the eye and confessed that I'd once traveled across the Sahara with a band of gypsies. And another time, I'd allowed a family of midget circus performers to have their collective way with me on the floor of an elephant's tent. He sipped his beer and nodded. His eyes roamed over me. I leaned forward, allowing him a better view of my breasts.

When I paused for a breath, Cole asked me what Marianna Marissa Delacroix was looking for tonight. I slid my hand just under the cuff of his shorts, bit my lower lip, and told him I thought he knew what I was looking for.

He paid our bill, led me into the street, and hailed a carriage. We sat behind the driver, watching the horse's ass sway sensuously. We kissed, his beard like a razor on my cheek. Then I went down on him. I wrapped my right hand around the shaft of his cock while cupping his balls with my left. I bobbed up and down and drizzled saliva. I jacked him slowly while my tongue and lips sucked and nurtured his sweetness.

His hips began to rock until he was fucking my mouth. I licked from the base to the tip and teased his pee-hole until he pulled away from the intensity of it. I pumped the shaft while flicking relentlessly at that most sensitive spot on the underside of the head. I felt his balls rise and tighten.

After I swallowed every drop, I kissed Cole on the cheek and told the driver to let me off. I caught the streetcar and went back to my place to become Lanie again.

Carson McCullers was right. The heart is indeed a lonely hunter.

Shortly before final exams, we planned an escape to the Royal Orleans for one last fling before semester break. I took extra care in preparing for our tryst, shaving and scenting myself. I dressed elegantly in a little black dress and pearls. Underneath, I wore black thigh-highs and a black thong. I wanted to make it an evening he'd never forget.

We dined at Galatoire's, beginning with shrimp and crawfish. I ordered pompano *en croûte* and J chose the stuffed flounder. We each drank a bottle of wine and stumbled to our retreat arm in arm. The night was cool and crisp; Thanksgiving and Christmas were just around the corner. I flung open the doors to our balcony again, inhaling the aroma of that bitch, New Orleans. I undressed and danced out there while he sipped brandy and watched from inside. When I was naked, save for my thong, he was on me, his erection like an iron pipe in his suit pants. He sat on a chair and pulled me across his lap. I looked up at him and smiled a nasty smile. This was a game we hadn't played before.

We kissed, then he began to massage my buttocks, telling me how much he loved my ass. His fingers played games with the straps of my thong, then retreated. I moaned, and he took it as a sign and brought his open hand down hard against my flesh. The mixture of pain and pleasure nearly overwhelmed me.

I grunted, "Oh yes."

His touch told me to lift my hips and, in a flash, my thong was gone.

"I want your ass," he breathed.

"It's yours," I murmured.

He worked my thighs apart. I found leverage against his knee and ground against him. His hand opened my pussy lips and probed the slit, coming up slick. Two fingers dallied inside my cunt, playing me like an instrument. Squishy pussy sounds and the scent of arousal filled the air. People walked below us, paying no mind, lost in their own lives. His forefinger circled my clit, causing me to squirm. Then those slippery fingers strummed the deep furrow between my ass cheeks and instinctively, I clenched. His slap across my butt cheeks was firm and loving. I cried out like the naughty girl I was.

He pushed me off his lap onto the cool cement of the balcony. He lowered his mouth to me while I swayed before him, my ass thrust high. His mouth and tongue found a trail to my asshole. In my mind's eye, I watched him tease the brown pucker. I clenched again when his tongue entered me and his hand delivered another well-deserved swat. Then his mouth became my salvation. His tongue searched and probed my darkness, eliciting sensations I'd never felt before. I pushed against him, wanting to swallow him up. He brought me to the edge, then retreated.

Now, well lubricated and leaking girl-cum down my thighs, I was directed back onto his lap. Gently, a finger, not a tongue, plied my asshole. He entered virgin territory and, instead of withdrawing, I pushed back again, seeking relief.

"That's my girl," he said.

I accepted him and felt his finger work deep, opening me, stretching me. Saliva drooled from my open mouth and formed a pool at his feet. I reached for my clit, needy for release.

He pushed my hand away. "I'll tell you when."

"Please . . ."

"Not yet."

He pumped in and out, one finger up my ass and two inside my cunt. I lost the ability to reason, gave into the pure lust of the moment. He must have sensed my orgasm drawing near, because he withdrew and directed me off of his lap and back inside our suite.

He held me and whispered sweetly, "How do you want it?"

I looked up at him, face shining in the street lights, eyes hungry and needy, and told him I wanted it in my ass and that I wouldn't settle for anything less.

It was my first time to be fucked in the ass, certainly not my last, but I remember it like I remember the first time a boy touched my breasts, or finger-fucked me, or the first time I gave a boy a hand job or a blow job, or let him fuck me in the backseat of his car.

J leaned me over the arm of the Queen Anne sofa, my toes barely touching the ground, my ass high in the air. He retrieved lubricant from the top drawer of the nightstand next to our bed and applied a generous handful to my ass. He kneaded my cheeks as if he were kneading a loaf of bread. I felt something hard press between them—a vibrator we'd bought at a novelty store in The Quarter. Its slippery tip prodded my rosebud.

J spoke to me, whispering softly in my ear, "We'll take this slow. I want you to invite me in. I will not force it."

In a far corner of my mind, it occurred to me that he'd probably done this before with another student, with many of us over the years. But I didn't care. I was his choice of the moment and I wanted what he had to give. I felt myself being slowly pried apart as the vibe invaded my dark center.

J's words, with their carefully modulated pace, continued, "Imagine, Lanie, that your ass is loving this vibe as your pussy might. You open yourself to it; you invite it inside as you would invite your own finger or a lover's cock. You take it a little at a time. That's it . . . draw it inside . . . invite it inside. Yes, that's my girl."

Guided by his experience and patience, I accepted that vibe as a mouth accepts a nipple, as an urn accepts its due. I allowed it to fill me and grace me with its presence. In and out, he worked and I rode that plastic cock like a stallion. I felt nasty and redeemed of my nastiness, all at once. I felt dark, yet knew that vibe was the way to the light. I felt a quickening between my legs and was awash with the syrup of my sex.

"Oh, baby, I'm going to come."

J slowed to a halt. "Not yet, my girl. I'm going to take it out and give you my cock to come on."

"Oh, God."

Never was an emptiness so vast as when he withdrew, but no sooner than the vibe was cast aside than I felt his cock, hard and needy, at my opening.

"Pull me in, baby. Open the door and pull me in."

Then I was full again, filled again. And it was my J, my sweet J, filling me, his breath hot on my neck. I began to spasm after only a stroke or two, an orgasm deeper, darker, earthier than anything I'd ever experienced. It was only the first of several, as the relief came in wave after wave, each climax harder and more powerful than the last. My pussy, my ass, my pussy, my ass . . . it was all just Lanie. I whimpered, I cried, I screamed. I shook and shuddered and ground my teeth together in sweet ecstasy.

When I was finished and my legs were too weak to stand, J was still hard inside me. Slowly, he exited and I reached behind to spread myself for him. I looked over my shoulder and saw him stroking his cock. I heard him shout my name and felt the splatters of his cum on my ass and thighs and lower back.

"Oh baby, oh baby, oh baby."

And then his hairy chest pressed against me and our lips met and we kissed, tongues chasing each other like feral animals.

Yes, yes, yes.

Yes, there in our suite in the Royal Orleans, kissing and teetering on the edge of a ragged New Orleans night, on the eve of finals and Christmas break, we were oblivious to the fact that our lives were about to change and things would never be like this again.

I Saw the Light

I waved and he waved back, the curly headed one with the "Dirty Road" T-shirt. Pete, the guitar player, said I should show him my tits. I told him I wasn't that kind of girl.

But I did throw him a kiss. His name was Alec and he and his two buddies were on vacation from their jobs at a tire factory in Ohio. They'd attended every concert on our two-week tour through Tennessee, Kentucky, and Indiana. They'd followed our bus everywhere we went. We'd gotten to know them by now.

Alec saluted from behind the dirty windshield of their Ford pickup.

"I love you," I mouthed the words and he and his buddies laughed. They punched him on the shoulders.

I turned away and settled into my seat, intent on a few hours sleep before our concert that night. Scattered about the bus, guys in the band picked out songs, played cards, and shot the shit. Beside me, Bobby Earl rolled another joint. He'd bought some dynamite weed for the tour.

"After I finish this, I'm going to take you to the bathroom and fuck you good," he said from under the Stetson pulled low onto his brow. He said it like he was entitled, which he was. After all, it was his band—Bobby Earl and the Truck Stop Daddies.

"I'm tired," I said.

"And I'm horny as . . ."

"I know, a Texas toad."

"Something like that."

"I'll give you a blow job right now."

His eyes widened behind the reefer's red glow. He looked around. "I reckon no one would mind."

He put his hand on the back of my head and pushed my face into his crotch.

I unzipped his jeans, took his fat cock into my mouth, and began to suck. I had him bucking like a stallion out of the chute in no time flat. I got every drop.

It's something you get good at when you're the only chick in the band.

I'm not really in the band, but I'm the opening act and I sing harmony on a few songs with the band.

Bobby saw me playing the bars in Austin and liked what he saw. It was too good a gig to turn down. I was thirty-four years old, I had cellulite where I used to have muscle, and I'd been kicking around the scene since I was sixteen. I could still belt it out, still pick a mean guitar, and still two-step with the best, but I needed a change. I needed a place to sleep, three hots a day, and all the smoke I could toke. I needed some green in my jeans.

Most of all, I needed a break from barroom hustlers and drugstore cowboys, from Larry Mahan wannabes and Ray Wylie Hubbard look-a-likes.

It had been a few years since Bobby Earl's last Top 40 hit, but he was still a Texas Outlaw icon, right up there with Willie and Townes and Stevie Ray Vaughan. He played theatres and auditoriums and the occasional convention center. He packed them in to hear his songs—"The Dirty Road," "Forever Texas," "Flat-Busted Floozy," and all the rest.

It beat the hell out of smoky barrooms and honky-tonk heroes.

I understood the tradeoff. I'd be Bobby's girl for the tour. That's the way it went. That's the business. That's what it means to be a blonde chick singer with a nice ass and decent tits.

It really was a dirty road.

I got over it about the time my first paycheck cleared.

"No way your daddy is a preacher."

"Why would I lie about something like that?" Alec asked.

"I don't know. I'm used to guys lying about everything."

After the concert that night, Bobby invited those boys from Ohio to join us for the after-party. He thought it was cool that they were following us around. He gave them free beer and T-shirts. He autographed CDs. After the party wound down, Bobby passed out and Alec and I went next door to the all-night diner.

The waitress called us both *honey* and kept our coffee cups full. Her eyes looked like ten miles of bad road.

"Well, I'm not a liar," Alec said.

"I can see that."

"How about your family?"

"My daddy worked the rigs in Corpus Christi Bay. He'd get off at midnight, drink till dawn, and sleep the morning away. Momma was a waitress."

He winced. "That's tough. But I can hear it in your songs. I love 'Third Shift.'"

I'd written that song in an alley my first week in Austin years earlier. I sang it the first time on the sidewalk, the next day for nickels and dimes. These days, I sang it to crowds who knew every word by heart.

"Yeah, I like that song too."

Alec stared into his coffee. "I can't believe I'm sitting here with Shana Shackleford. The other guys had decided to follow the tour before we even knew you'd joined. I was on the fence until I heard you were traveling with the band."

I smiled at him. He was just twenty-one, skinny as a birch sapling, and hard as nails. I liked his soft, brown eyes.

"Well, I'm glad you're here," I told him.

"My favorite song of yours is that gospel tune, 'The River.'"

"Preacher's son, it figures."

"Were you really baptized in a river?"

"Honey, I ain't never been baptized."

His eyes narrowed. "You're not one with the Lord?"

The Lord was about the only one I hadn't been one with, but I didn't tell Alec. Instead, I patted his hand. "Not exactly."

"But in your song . . ."

"It's just a song, Alec."

"But the feelings are real."

"I guess. I couldn't have written it otherwise, but it never really happened."

He stared out the window, watching the trucks roll by like steel stallions. "I'll pray for your soul."

I would've slapped him if I thought it was a line. Believe me, I've had my share of born again prophylactic-pushing proselytizers. Come two in the morning, when the lights go down and the chairs are on the tables, they just want to fuck like all the other midnight ramblers. That one-on-one relationship they've got with Jesus, that little woman back home, that fancy job at the Christian corporation—come two in the morning, when the lights go down, they'll trade it all for a slice of pussy pie.

But I could see this wasn't a line for Alec. He really did mean to pray for my sorry soul. More than that, he really thought it would make a difference.

"Well, I appreciate that," I told him.

He left a ten on the table for the coffee. I left five more for the waitress.

I knew how much tips meant to a working girl.

Bobby Earl was a tiger in the morning. When he rolled over, nuzzled his three-day growth into the back of my neck, and spooned me, I knew it was time to rise and shine. He had a hard-on like a bulwark fencepost you could hang a five-rail gate from.

"I love the smell of Shana in the morning," he whispered in my ear.

I wriggled out of my panties and T-shirt. I guided his hand to my breasts. He fondled and humped. We had the Presidential Suite at the Knoxville Comfort Inn. From what I could see from under the sheets, we shared it with Johnnie Walker, Jack Daniels, and George Dickel. Mostly empties.

I flipped over, threw a leg across Bobby's big, hairy belly, and straddled him. I dragged my nipples down his chest.

"Hold on," he said.

He reached into the drawer of the nightstand, then searched for and found a bottle of Astroglide. He rubbed it onto and between my breasts. When I was slipperier than a pig in the mud, I slid his cock into my cleavage. I clasped my breasts around him and he commenced to thrust.

"You like that, baby?"

"You know I do," he said.

I bit my lower lip, sexy like, and pinched my nipples. "Fuck my titties, Bobby," I whispered between clenched teeth.

He didn't have to be told twice.

I guessed him to be forty-five. He'd packed on a few pounds, a few wrinkles, and a few gray hairs since his infamous and groundbreaking "Dirty Road" tour. But he was still cute in a pudgy, grizzled sort of way. As a girl living at home with my folks, I'd kept his poster on the wall of our double-wide. You had to look hard to find the Bobby Earl on that poster in the man lying beneath me.

"Oh, yeah," he groaned and squirmed.

I felt it hot and sticky. I milked him like a farmer milking a heifer. "Give it to me, Bobby. Give it to me."

When it was over, he said, "Girl, you are something." He panted like a house afire.

I kissed him on the cheek and settled next to him, both of us staring at the ceiling. Hot and sticky turned to cold and damp real quick.

He lit us both a smoke before his cell phone rang. He checked the LCD, turned, and sat on the edge of the bed with his back to me. "It's Maggie," he said over his shoulder.

The wife.

"I'm good, honey. How 'bout you? How're the girls?"

I slid off the other side of the bed. I wiped down with toilet paper and took a long, hot shower.

We wrapped up the tour at IU in Bloomington to a sold-out crowd. It was one of those times. My voice filled the auditorium; my guitar raged. It's not something you control.

I sang "Third Shift" and "The River," of course. I sang that song about Lillie and Billy from Nacogdoches, don't you know. I told the story about the fellow from Waco who bought my first CD online and how I took it to him in person only to have his wife meet me at the door with a shotgun. She told me I'd have to come through her first. Now, that was a true story.

After I got the crowd warmed up, the band took the stage.

Bobby's gravelly voice rocked them and they sang along and danced in the aisles. When he and I did our "Blue Bonnet Highway" duet, those college kids went wild. While I sang harmony on "Beef Brisket Breakdown," a girl in the front row threw herself onto the stage. Bobby let her touch his Luccheses before the ushers dragged her away.

I spied Alec and his friends, five rows back. I pointed them out to Bobby and he made a big deal, telling the crowd about how these boys from Ohio had been shadowing us all week.

They received a standing ovation for their loyalty and dedication.

When I took my final bow, following the band's second encore (an unbelievable new version of one of Bobby's earliest hits, "Pistols on the Table," complete with electric guitar riffs and a drum solo), Alec pointed at me, signaling he wanted talk.

Bobby and the boys were off to a party at a local DJ's house and didn't even notice when I slipped away.

I met Alec on the square outside the Hilton Garden Inn, higher than the Texas sky on post-concert adrenaline.

"You guys were great tonight," he said.

I offered him a tug of my Dickel's, which he turned down because he didn't drink.

"Some nights are better than others," I said.

He took my hand. "You ever been on this campus?"

"Nossir."

"It's pretty. Let's take a walk."

I tossed the Dickel's into a trash can.

The warm, spring air settled over us like a blanket. The dogwoods and cherry trees were in bloom. The daffodils and tulips pushed through the heavy Midwestern loam, their fragrance filling the air. We passed through Dunn Meadow and wandered out back where huge old maples and oaks reached toward the star-filled sky. This late on a week night, even the students had deserted the brick walkways.

"My cousin went to school here," Alec explained. "I used to visit. It's a pretty campus. I wish you could see it in daylight."

"This is the furthest north I've ever been," I confessed.

"How do you like it?"

"This is nice enough, but I miss Texas."

We walked in front of what a sign identified as the Chemistry Building. He guided me across the street.

"I prayed for your soul today," Alec said.

I could hear the bubble of a stream. We descended a stairway. "I'll take all the help I can get."

"Over here," he said.

A small limestone building surrounded by an old cemetery loomed before us. "What's this?"

"This is the chapel. This is where I came to pray for you."

He tried the door. It opened and we stepped inside. Rows of hardwood pews lined both sides of a narrow aisle. Up front was a stage and lectern. Behind and above the lectern, an icon of Christ our Savior on the cross was illuminated by a dim light.

"It's pretty," I said.

We sat in the front pew. It seemed a little less worn than the others. Alec slipped one arm across my shoulders and placed a hand on my knee. He stared into my eyes, the most earnest look I'd ever seen playing across his face.

"Can you feel the presence of the Lord?" he asked.

I sighed deeply. "Not so much."

"He's here with us, Shana."

"If you say so."

"He'll forgive you for your sins. All you have to do is accept him in your heart."

"Look, Alec, you're a real sweet guy, but you're over your head here."

He clasped my hand in his. "Shana, you have a gift for music and you write songs that lift people's hearts. I know God loves you."

I stood and took a step away. I straightened my skirt with the "Snowin' on Raton" lyrics embroidered on it. "Do you have a girlfriend, Alec?"

"What?"

"You heard me. Do you have a girlfriend?"

"No one special."

"Well, that explains it. You need a girlfriend."

"What do you mean?"

"You've got a crush on me and the only way you know how to express it is by trying to save me."

He looked like he'd been run over by a truck. "I'm just concerned about your soul. My daddy says eternity is a long time to burn."

I couldn't escape those eyes. I reached out and touched his cheek. I brushed a lock of hair off his forehead. Then I leaned forward and pulled his face into my bosom. "You've never been with girl, have you?"

He hugged me to him. "No, ma'am. We believe in abstinence until marriage."

My mouth went suddenly dry. I held his face, his beautiful, unblemished face, in my hands. "You sweet boy."

He licked his lips. "We should probably go."

I brought his hand up under my skirt and pressed it between my legs. "We're not going anywhere."

Years before, there'd been a rodeo cowboy up Amarillo way. He rode bulls and wrestled steers. For five days, we locked ourselves away in a room at the Highway 87 Motor Inn. We lived on Cheetos and Diet Coke—and love, sweet love. When we finally stepped out into that bright Texas sun, we had no idea that good-bye kiss was forever. He went north and I went south and we never saw each other again.

That hard Amarillo highway ran the entire length of Texas.

I hadn't felt what I was feeling for Alec since that cowboy.

I pushed Alec down on the carpet in the aisle between the pews.

I stood over him, removed my blouse and bra, my boots and skirt, and my panties. I folded everything neatly and placed the pile on the lectern beneath that icon of Jesus of Bethlehem. Alec watched every move.

I knelt next to him and unbuttoned his shirt.

"Shana, please," he said.

I ran my fingertips over his hairless chest. I pinched a nipple. "Please, what?"

"I can't do this."

I stroked his cock through stiff denim. "Honey, this is what a man and a woman do."

He swallowed hard. "But we're not married."

I unloosed his belt, unzipped him, and pulled his jeans off his skinny hips. I kissed his lips, our tongues dueling. He was slippery, long and hard in my hand. I stroked him slowly, my eyes locked on his.

"This is right and good, Alec. Can't you feel it?"

He had an iron will, but I meant to break it. "I don't know. I just don't know."

"Yes you do." I guided his hand to my breast. He squeezed, tentatively. I lowered a nipple to his mouth. He licked and suckled like a babe.

His resistance was weakening. "You're so beautiful," he said.

I returned the favor, taking him into my mouth. When I withdrew, a gossamer string of pre-cum stretched from his cockhead to my lips. "And so are you."

I sat across his flat belly, his abs like a washboard. He stared up at me, his lower lip trembling. "What will God think?"

"If he's the God you think he is, he won't bat an eye at this."

I squatted, lowered myself, and felt him enter me.

"Oh my God," he gasped.

"I got this. Just go with it." I began to rock. Oh, yeah, it had been a while.

But no sooner had I found a rhythm than he gushed. I squeezed him inside and kissed him gently.

"I'm sorry," he said.

"I'm not, baby."

I knew there was more where that came from. I stayed put, kissing him, feeling his hands on my thighs and backside. After a while, I began to rock again. Angels sang on high. Cherubs floated in the air, strumming harps. Somewhere, not far away, the Beast grunted, snorted fire, but I paid that son of a bitch no mind.

I came, belly clenching, thighs shuddering, eyes locked on that crucifix.

As Alec spurted for the second time that night, I silently mouthed the words, "Thank you, Jesus."

He closed his eyes. "Amen," he whispered.

The next morning, I packed up while Bobby slept off the whisky and the tour. I could probably have stayed on, hung with the band, and got invited for the next one, but I had other things on my mind.

I grabbed a cup of coffee at Starbucks and used a public computer in the Union to run an Internet search. I turned up five guys named Rowdy Yates. Only one of them lived in Texas. I found a newspaper article about him through Google. He wasn't riding bulls or wrestling steers anymore, but he still worked the rodeo. He'd become a highly sought after rodeo clown.

I got his number from information in San Marcos. I recognized the voice on the machine right away. There wasn't any mention of a wife or girlfriend, so I left a message. I said he should call back if he ever thought about that Highway 87 Motor Inn in Amarillo and the girl he'd been with there, so long ago.

I caught a ride from a trucker headed south, my guitar on my back, my bag in my hand, and my nose to the wind. I figured to make Texas by nightfall the next day.

While me and that trucker listened to the radio and sang those good old country tunes, I jotted out a note to Bobby. I wrote, "Thanks and good luck." I advised him to spend more time with his wife and family. I said to go easy on the dope and the booze. I told him what no one else would—he wasn't getting any younger.

I even said a silent prayer for Alec, not that he needed it, and not that I thought anyone was listening. It just seemed like the right thing to do.

About the time we reached Louisville, my cell phone rang. It was that cowboy down San Marcos way.

Fridays Without

It began as a joke. They were at Starbucks on one of those heavy, summer mornings in North Carolina for Charis, Mary, and Renee's "Mommy's Morning Out," drinking lattes and talking about their plans for the upcoming weekend. Kate, the only single in the crowd, was always amazed to hear how busy these married women were—in-laws to manage, gardens and husbands to tend, and soccer matches and softball games to cheer at. For her part, Kate used the weekends to recharge from her job at the public library. It surprised everyone when Charis, the daughter of a southern Baptist preacher, blurted out that what she hoped for most over the weekend was the chance to spend a little "cootchy-coo" time with her hubby, Todd.

"Why, Charis, bless your heart," Renee, the raven-haired vamp of the group, drawled. "Todd not taking proper care of you?"

"Well, he works most of the time, and when he is home, there's grass to cut and the kids and the dogs. Why, it's been at least a month since . . ." Here Charis's voice trailed off.

Kate made a little "eek" face, but didn't say that it had been at least a year since she'd even been on a date. It wasn't as easy to meet guys out in the "real world" as it was in college.

Mary patted Charis's hand and said, "I know how it is. The last time Patrick and I tried to get it on, our three-year-old walked in on us. I swear, my legs were in the air and Patrick was just hitting his stride."

"Don't talk it about it," Charis said. "That just makes it worse."

Renee leaned in. All about them, people cut business deals and juiced up on caffeine. "Sugar, if I want my man's attention, I wear a short skirt and lose my underpants. In fact, I do it every Friday."

Charis gasped. "You mean . . ."

"That's right," Renee said. "No panties. When Ray comes home, I get him a cold one and we park the kids in front of the TV. While he enjoys his beer on the deck, I cross and uncross my legs. While I make dinner, I reach high into the cabinet or bend over to the refrigerator. I give him a little show and by bedtime, I guarantee he's not thinking about sleeping."

Kate had to cover her smile. It wasn't all that hard to get Ray's attention. She'd caught him staring at her breasts on more than one occasion, and at the last block party, he'd asked if she'd ever been with an older, married man.

She pushed her glasses up on her nose. "So, right now, you're not . . ."

"No, ma'am," Renee answered. "I always go without on Fridays."

Kate, Mary, and Charis stared at each other for a moment, then broke out laughing.

"Well," Mary said. "I'd be willing to give it a try. I'm not exactly getting as much of Dave's attention as I'd like."

"It would certainly give Todd something to think about," Charis said. "It would be cooler, too, on these hot summer days."

"We should all do this," Renee said. "We should go without on Fridays."

Mary nodded. "I guess it couldn't hurt."

Charis's eyes were far away. "It might even be fun."

Kate felt a red burn on her cheeks. The idea of running around without panties both embarrassed and intrigued her. "And would we wear short skirts?"

"What's the point if you don't?" Renee replied.

"I mean, at a library, I don't know . . ."

Charis put an arm around Kate's shoulder. "Don't be so shy, sugar. Maybe you'll meet a gentleman."

The women giggled. They liked having fun at Kate's expense, especially when it came to teasing her about her shyness. And men.

Kate's blush deepened. "Okay, I guess, I mean, I suppose I could do it."

Renee extended her hand. "C'mon, are we in or aren't we? Fridays without!"

Mary, Charis, and Kate placed their hands on Renee's. A group shake. "Fridays without," they said in unison.

That had been ten years ago. In the interim, Charis and Todd had divorced, Renee and Ray had joined a swingers' club, Mary and Dave had gone on to have two more kids, and Kate had finished her master's and taken a job in Washington, DC. In a quiet government building not far from the White House, she stood sentry over dusty classics and national treasures. She remained single and stayed in touch with her old friends by phone and e-mail. After all this time, it still came up now and then.

The women liked to joke about the time in their lives when they'd gone without on Fridays. Kate remained silent, refusing to confess that she, alone among her old friends, continued the practice. She couldn't say why, other than she enjoyed the cool freedom beneath a dress or skirt.

And there was something else, something her shyness made difficult to admit even to herself. Going without was a little—well, a little exciting. The secret knowledge that only a thin veneer of fabric prevented exposure of her most private parts to strangers often left her moist by the end of the day.

Summers in DC were usually languid and slow, except for the tourists, who were rarely interested in Kate's little library, anyway. But with a presidential election and an economic meltdown underway, this summer was anything but slow. Congressmen and lobbyists cluttered the National Mall, reporters clogged the White House gates, and more than a few academic types descended on Kate's space to research parallels to what many considered a historic moment.

She'd overheard them talking. The current economic crisis was comparable to the Great Depression. The potential for the election of the country's first black president had its roots in the 1960s.

Most of the visitors to her library were frumpy old professors with balding heads, frayed collars, and elbow patches. But one man drew Kate's attention. He was tall and dark, early to mid-fifties—fifteen years older than her, she guessed. Unlike the others, he was fit and lean and wore his shirts outside his jeans. He sported a goatee and a diamond earring, and pulled his longish hair into a ponytail.

Kate caught him looking on more than one occasion.

Once, she dropped to a squat to retrieve a sheaf of dusty papers from a lower shelf. From a nearby carrel, Mr. Goatee peered unabashedly at the dark V between her knees. She stood, pressed her skirt down, and went about her business.

Another time, she was leaning over her computer, engaged in a Google search, when he appeared at the counter with a question about Lincoln's first inaugural address. Although the blouse she wore was modest enough, her top had opened to offer a glimpse of cleavage. Mr. Tight Jeans's eyes found the offering in an instant and Kate had to resist the urge to close the blouse about her throat. Instead, she met his mahogany eyes square on and answered his inquiry in her most professional manner.

But the time that stood out the most occurred late on a Friday afternoon. She teetered high on a ladder to restore a volume about the 1880's bank crisis to its rightful place. As she stretched for position, she sensed movement below. Directly below her and looking up with a bemused grin was Mr. Brown Eyes.

"I thought you might like to put this one away too," he said. "I mean, while you're up there."

Kate felt that familiar flush. Because it was Friday, she wore no panties, not even nylons under her floral-pattern dress. She was fully exposed and had little doubt the man had seen it all.

"Well," she said.

He continued to gaze steadily as he handed her the book in question. "I can hold the ladder, if that will help."

"No, thank you," she replied in a measured tone. "I can manage just fine."

The next week, Kate's life followed its usual routine. Over the weekend, she dashed about, cleaning her apartment and checking errands off her list.

After work on Monday, she walked from the library to Dupont Circle, where she dined alone at an Italian restaurant. On Tuesday evening, she worked out at the gym before grabbing sushi at a little spot on K Street. After leaving the library on Wednesday, she met with her book club at a coffee shop in Georgetown. Thursday, she hit the gym again and dined at a French bistro near the Capitol with a former coworker, a gay man in the midst of a midlife crisis.

Back at her apartment that evening, she undressed, indulged in a single glass of red wine, selected a thin volume of erotica from her bookshelf, and using a discreet, pink vibrator, masturbated to the images conjured up by her favorite story.

The story was about a woman who discovers the man in the apartment across the way spying on her through a telescope. At first, the woman is outraged, but then the thought of being on display begins to appeal to her. Over time, the woman and the man engage in an intricate courtship. She flits about her apartment in various stages of undress, dances the rumba naked under the man's watchful eye, and even touches herself for their mutual benefit.

The story never failed to work its magic and it wasn't long before Kate was bouncing on her sofa, her vibrator buzzing.

After pushing herself to a gut-clenching orgasm, she collapsed in a puddle and felt the familiar loneliness wash over her that often followed her Thursday-evening ritual. As she neared age forty, was this all that remained? A glass of wine and a vibrator?

She feared it was so.

Although the workouts kept her fit and she was attractive enough beneath her bangs and behind her glasses, she'd never really connected with any of the men she'd dated over the years. Eventually, the conversation turned dull and the sex mechanical. Stick this here, move this there.

Nothing like the sex in her favorite story.

Kate wiped her vibrator clean and returned it with a kiss to its velvet holder. She turned off the reading lamp, shuffled across her carpet to the floor-to-ceiling window, and flung open the curtains. Her nakedness hidden in the shadows, she peered across a courtyard into the apartments of an adjacent building. Most of the rooms were darkened. Only a few were lit well enough to offer a glimpse of the lives that took place within.

She sighed. No one returned her gaze.

The next morning, she was deep in the stacks, returning books to their rightful places, when she felt a presence behind her.

"Excuse me," he said. "I've been looking for those."

She turned to face Mr. Ponytail. He rested against a nearby table, his long lean legs stretched out before him.

"Oh, you startled me," she managed.

He extended a hand. "I suppose I should introduce myself. I'm Michael Dane, a history professor from Greenwich College."

"I'm Kate Summers, the librarian, but I guess you knew that."

"I offered to steady your ladder last week. Remember?"

She tried not to wince. "I remember."

"Anyway, I'm researching a book. I'm looking for letters written by Union soldiers during the Civil War."

"You're in the right area."

He grinned mischievously and pointed to the highest shelf. "I think that's the collection I'm looking for. I hate to ask, but is there any chance . . ."

Kate shot a look at the leather-bound volume to which he pointed. "Do you need it right away?"

"I'd like to see it as soon as possible. The book, I mean."

"The book. Well, of course, the book."

"I suppose I could get it myself, except . . ."

"No, that's against policy. Liability issues, you know."

He was no longer grinning and his dark eyes seemed to penetrate her soul. "So, you wouldn't mind . . ."

Kate sensed that this was about much more than a book, but felt she had little choice but to go along. "Not a bit. It's my job, after all."

"Then I'd really like to see it. The book, that is. I'll wait here, if that's all right."

"That's fine."

Then, he reached out and placed his hand on her forearm. "I know it's fine, but do you really want me to? That's the question."

"Want you to . . ."

His eyes bored into her. "Wait at the bottom of the ladder and watch while you go up."

Suddenly, what had started out as an innocent flirtation had taken a turn. They were alone in a deserted part of the library, playing an indelicate game. She felt loose and uncertain inside and had to fight to maintain her composure.

After a moment, in an almost inaudible whisper, she said, "Yes."

"Yes, what?"

The words welled up from deep inside. "Yes, I really want you to watch me climb the ladder."

"Then I'll stand right here," he assured her.

"It'll only take a sec."

"Take your time."

As she mounted the ladder and began to climb, she sensed his eyes on her calves, then her thighs, and then her firm bottom—the beneficiary of those twice-a-week sessions on the Stairmaster.

"There, that's pretty close," he said. "Just a little to the left."

Her hands were sweaty and that secret place between her legs was sticky. This was unladylike, bordering on the obscene.

But she couldn't resist.

She leaned, bent slightly at the waist, and felt her skirt rise well over her knees.

"Yes, right there," Michael Dane said. She thought he sounded a little breathy.

"Is that what you're looking for?"

"That's exactly what I'm looking for."

She clutched the heavy book to her breast and began the journey down. He shifted position for a straight up-the-skirt view. She could have called him on it, slapped him across the face, or scolded him.

But she didn't.

By the time she reached the bottom rung, the stickiness between her legs had become a sheen on her thighs.

"Thanks," he said when she handed him the book. "That was nice. Very nice."

She couldn't face him. Her eyes dropped and inadvertently fixed on his crotch. There was no mistaking the erection pulsing in his jeans.

"No problem," she managed. "I'm glad to do it."

He took her hand. "Then maybe you'd like to have dinner tonight."

It crossed her mind that they'd probably miss her at the Thai restaurant where she usually picked up take-out on Friday evenings.

"I'll have to check my calendar," she said, trying to maintain at least a semblance of decency. "But, sure, I'm free. I mean, where did you have in mind? What time were you thinking?"

That evening over dinner, he said that if she trusted him, he'd never place her in danger. He promised to be discreet.

Then he exposed her for the first time.

1776 in Georgetown was the kind of restaurant where politicians made deals, parents dined when they visited their children at college, and young couples fell in love. As he sipped an expensive Cabernet Sauvignon and dined on rack of lamb, Michael Dane suggested that Kate remove her bra and release the top button of her silk blouse.

Her hands trembled in the ladies' room.

When the middle-aged waiter took her order, her brownish-pink aureoles rolled and flashed beneath a sea of white. The waiter's eyes devoured her. And Michael smiled knowingly.

Under the table, he nudged a hand up her skirt, pushed her legs open, and grazed her thighs with his fingertips. An older woman at a nearby table raised an eyebrow.

On the cab ride to her apartment, he asked her to remove her top. While the cabbie stole furtive glances in the rearview, Michael sucked her bared breasts. Passersby and pedestrians gawked, then giggled or shook their heads in disbelief.

He allowed her to wear the blouse to her apartment, but insisted she leave it unbuttoned. The wispy blonde in a T-shirt and shorts with whom they shared the elevator pretended not to notice Kate's disheveled appearance or the wet spot blooming on her companion's trousers.

Once behind closed doors, he took his time opening the curtains, but leaving the lights off for what he characterized as their "initial encounter." He reclined on the sofa and directed her to undress in front of the window where she'd stood alone a few days earlier. She removed one article at a time—the blouse, the skirt, the thigh-high nylons. When she was naked, except for her glasses, he told her to turn around.

"Bend over," he said.

She leaned, steadying herself with a hand on the window. There would be a smudge in the morning.

"Show me," he whispered.

She rested her forehead against the glass and clasped her ass cheeks in her hands. She lifted and separated.

She heard him stand, then felt his presence like she'd felt it in the stacks earlier in the day. There was a rustle and a click, and then his penlight reflected in the window. She squinted at its brightness as he examined her, the pucker and the crinkle, the folds and rilles. She hadn't expected the light.

"Lovely, but you need to shave," he said.

"Down there?"

"Of course, down here. Touch yourself."

"You mean . . ."

"Your clit."

"Oh my God."

"It's swollen to the size of an olive."

"Oh my."

"Show me some pink."

"You mean . . ."

"You know what I mean."

She opened her pussy lips and felt the probing light. His breathing quickened as he inspected every nook and cranny.

"Now your asshole," he whispered.

She planted her feet wider, thrust her hips out farther, and tugged at her sensitive flesh. The penlight's reflection in the window moved.

"That's beautiful," he said. The light flashed off. He stood and leaned against her, pressing her forehead against the cool glass. His breath was hot on her neck.

"Finger yourself," he said, his breath an explosion in her ear.

She didn't have to be told twice. She circled and rubbed.

She heard him move away. He settled on the sofa, unzipped his trousers, and withdrew a long, hard cock.

"I'm watching you," he whispered. "I'm watching you finger-fuck yourself."

"Oh, Michael."

"You're such a wanton slut beneath that proper façade."

She'd never thought of herself like that, but she liked hearing it—liked the way it made her feel more than she could have imagined.

Michael Dane's reflection stroked and tugged.

"The men across the way are watching you," he said. "They're pulling their dicks, wanting you."

It was unlikely that anyone could see inside the darkened room, but the idea drove her crazy. The squishy sounds of her pussy filled the air. Her knees were weak, her thighs trembling.

"Oh yeah," she moaned. "Oh yeah."

"Tell me when you're close," he said.

She thrust her pelvis in rhythm with her hand. She felt the pressure build at her core. "Almost, almost."

"Face me," he said.

She whirled and sunk to the floor, legs wide. One hand clutched a nipple, the other danced on her clit. Her eyes fixed on his cock, his movements a blur.

"Now, now, now," she gasped.

He stood and took two strides. As she ground out her orgasm, riding wave after wave, she watched him shoot once, twice, three times, rich and creamy, onto her chin and breasts.

She collapsed against the window. He leaned over and kissed her, their tongues swirling.

"Do you trust me?" he asked.

"Yes."

"Then I'll take you to heights you've never imagined."

Michael picked her up the following morning in a BMW convertible coupe. As instructed, she wore a T-shirt and a denim skirt that buttoned down the front. No bra or panties, even though it was Saturday, not Friday.

He wanted to visit the Civil War battlefield in Fredericksburg. Half an hour on the road, he pulled out to pass an eighteen-wheeler. As they came alongside the trucker, he told her to unbutton her skirt.

The trucker's jaw dropped when he peered into the convertible and saw Kate's creamy thighs and patch of black pubic hair. Behind her sunglasses, she was dizzy with lust.

Farther down the road, she flashed her breasts at a man and woman traveling in a minivan. The man winked and the woman appeared to chastise him.

While standing in line for lunch at a fast-food restaurant, Michael reached behind, pulled her skirt up, and caressed her ass. A single man seated across the way nearly choked on his Whopper.

That afternoon, instead of using the park's facilities, Kate squatted and pissed at the edge of the woods. Michael wiped her off with a Kleenex while two staid-looking women in casual Polo attire rubbernecked from the parking lot.

Just south of the city, he exited the highway. In a farmer's field, in the pink light of a setting sun, not twenty yards from the road, he fucked her for the first time. He positioned her on the hood of his car so she could see the cars passing by over his shoulder. She was so wet no foreplay was required—the whole day had been foreplay. She started coming the moment he pushed inside, one mind-shattering orgasm after another. Weak and shaky, she finished him on her hands and knees, clutching his hips and pulling him deep into her mouth.

They put the top up and she rode back to the city naked as the day she was born.

He would be in town for two more weeks before returning to upstate New York and a new class of freshmen history students. He was divorced with children from a previous marriage. There were other women in his life, but it would have surprised Kate to learn otherwise.

She followed his lead, knowing they'd have to make the best of their short time together.

One morning, while two white-haired professors debated the merits of a 19th century text on Andrew Johnson's impeachment, she sat at a nearby table pretending to sift through a book catalogue. While Michael watched from the shadows, she opened her legs wide enough to reveal the white panties beneath her black pinstripe skirt. It could have been absentmindedness.

First one professor, then the other, peeked over his reading glasses. By the time Michael whispered, "Enough," she'd soaked herself and perfumed the air with her pungent scent. As she walked away, she could hear the professors slapping each other's back and chortling, as if they were schoolboys getting away with something.

Michael met her in the 3rd floor ladies' room where she ground out a quickie while sitting on his lap.

One evening, at the hotel where Michael was staying, she stripped naked, except for her heels, and wrapped herself in his raincoat. While he sipped a drink in the lobby bar, she flashed the concierge from a second-floor landing. Afterwards, Michael took her to his room, led her onto the balcony overlooking Wisconsin Avenue, and dropped to his knees. She thrashed about on the tip of his tongue while pedestrians passed just yards below.

On another day, they took in a midday matinee at a downtown theatre. She jacked him off onto her breasts while another couple cast suspicious glances over their shoulders. She wore the sticky remains of his come all afternoon.

By the end of that first week, they'd grown even bolder. While riding the Metro back from a restaurant in Arlington, Michael reached deep into her slacks and fingered her hard. Across the aisle, a middle-aged woman looked up from her Washington Post, bit her lower lip, and squirmed. When Kate grunted out her climax, the woman squeezed her thighs together and made a whimpering sound.

On Saturday morning, Michael set his video camera on a tripod, attached the feed to her desktop computer, and streamed her first anal sex experience onto a website specializing in live amateurs. While the camera whirred and people all across the globe squinted at their screens, Kate knelt on her bed, her backside high in the air. Michael lubed her rectum and probed gently, first with his finger, then with a silicon plug. Only after she'd learned to relax and accept the intrusion did he stand over her and work his cockhead into her opening. Using a remote to adjust the camera angle, Michael shifted the focus to Kate's pretty face.

"Fuck me," she whispered to 1.2 million viewers, Kate the Librarian in her dark-rimmed glasses, "fuck me in the ass." When Michael buried himself, balls-deep, inside her, she screamed like a cat in heat.

The video clip received a 4.8 out of a possible five.

Two nights later, Michael appeared at her apartment door with a couple Kate had never seen before. She guessed the man was in his forties. His female Asian companion was young enough to be his daughter. Michael poured drinks while Kate ran hot water, perched herself on a kitchen counter, and applied shaving lather to her pubis. The young woman unfurled the man's soft, pink cock. While he watched Kate shave her pussy until it was as smooth as a wine glass, the Asian girl sucked and lapped. The man's breathing quickened, his face turned red, and he half-rose from his chair with a groan. His companion's red lips never left him, relishing every drop of her lover's nectar.

Their last night together, Michael rented a large suite at an uptown hotel. He pushed the furniture against the wall and placed a straight-backed chair in the middle of the room. He stripped Kate naked, bound her to the chair, and gagged her mouth with a thong. Her "safe" gesture was to shake her head right to left three times.

Strangers began to arrive. After a while, the room was crowded. They drank cocktails, talked in low voices, and ignored Kate, except for the occasional errant glimpse.

After a while, Michael announced that it was time for the show to begin. He produced an oddly shaped vibrator, long and thin with a bulbous head. He rubbed it first on her breasts, then slid it down her belly. While the crowd watched, Michael dipped the head into Kate's newly shorn pussy. The pleasure was excruciating. Ten to twenty pairs of eyes stared as Michael dipped in and out, then held the slickened instrument to her staining clit.

She tried to move, but the bindings were too tight. There was no escaping the persistent vibrations. The crowd drew closer, leaning in for a better look. A few of the men were stroking. One woman pressed a man's hand to the crotch of her jeans. Kate's first come ripped through her like a tornado through a trailer park. The crowd murmured.

Michael paused only briefly before continuing his efforts.

He plunged the vibe's head into her pussy and searched until he found that special spot. She strained against her bindings and a low moan escaped her. Her belly rippled, her thighs shuddered.

Twice more she came.

Too sensitive to continue, Kate gave him the sign. While she rested, legs splayed, pussy dripping, several of the men deposited their loads on her breasts. A woman, wearing a mask over her face, pressed her crotch to Kate's knee and humped like a dog. In the end, she bucked and wailed, only be led away by another masked woman.

When the strangers were gone, Michael loosened her bindings. He washed her off with a soft, warm cloth, then took her to bed where he held her close all night.

Over the next few months, they exchanged e-mails. He called twice. They talked about getting together for the holidays, but it never came to pass.

Kate's life settled into its old routine.

Then, one Friday evening in January, as a light snow fell on the city and the new President prepared to be sworn in, Kate turned on all the lights in her apartment, opened the curtains, and stood before the window. As usual, most of the apartments across the way were dark or closed up tight.

She'd gone without panties during the day, of course, but had worn heavy woolen slacks to protect her bare pussy from the cold. On a whim, she unbuckled the leather belt around her waist, undid the clasp, and wriggled free.

She turned so that her rump pressed against the window. She bent over, grabbed her buttocks, and opened herself wide.

"There," she said. "There."

Then, she turned again, and reached to close the curtains. She paused when she saw a man in jeans and T-shirt peering at her from across the courtyard. He hadn't been there when she'd looked earlier, or she hadn't noticed him. He raised a hand and waved.

Naked from the waist down, her first instinct was to draw the curtains tight and turn off the lights.

Instead, she held her ground, then raised her hand and returned the watcher's wave.

Snow continued to fall as they began their dance.

THIRD SHIFT

Tammi took the little balding man in the gray suit for just another stranger on the Mother Road. No doubt he was on his way to some place he'd just as soon not go, maybe a funeral or the forced sale of the family farm. She got her share of guys like that on the third shift at The Dixie Highway Truck Stop. She also got her share of horny truckers, touchy-feely salesmen, and drunk college boys on road trips.

Route 66 had a way of attracting losers and loners.

The little man ordered his coffee black, eggs sunny-side up, and toast plain. His fingernails were perfectly manicured, his remaining hair was impeccably trimmed, and he smelled clean and fresh as a sheet hung outside to dry on Tammi's clothesline.

"Thank you," he said. "Tammi."

He'd read her name tag—the one attached to where her left breast rested beneath the waitress uniform.

"You're welcome. Can I get you anything else?"

He spread a paper napkin across his lap and glanced around the diner. "You could sit and talk. I've been traveling all day and would appreciate your company."

Tammi gave him her sweetest smile. "I'm really not supposed to."

He nodded at the other waitress, Shana, across the way. She stood with a coffee pot in one hand, the other on her hip, flirting with a couple of truckers. "She going to tell on you?"

"Well . . ."

"I just want to talk."

"I really shouldn't."

The little man reached inside his suit coat pocket and produced a wallet. When he opened it, Tammi could see a roll of cash an inch wide. He peeled off a $100 bill and laid it on the table. He looked up at her with piercing gray eyes.

"I'm guessing you're pushing thirty-five, divorced, and just getting by. You're blonde and pretty and curvy beneath that dress, but you're not seeing anyone and know that time is running out. Especially, if you stay around here."

He'd pretty much read it right. She'd been on her own since her divorce from Dan six months earlier. Sometimes, after a day spent alone in her mobile home, The Dixie Highway didn't seem like such a bad place to work, after all.

"Okay, so what do you want?"

"A little conversation."

"Mister . . ."

"Avery, actually."

He peeled off another crisp hundred-dollar bill. Holy shit! It was more than she cleared in a week. She shot another look across the diner. Shana was still flirting with the truckers, but other than that, they'd hit a dead spot in the night.

"Well, all right," Tammi said. "But you don't have to give me money."

When she sat down, he pushed the bills across the table. "It's nothing really. Please, take it. I want you to."

"Mister, I don't know anything about you."

"Oh, I think you know me. I'm on the road and alone like everyone else who comes in here."

"So, what did you want to talk about?"

The man cut his eggs in precise halves, then dipped the corner of his toast into the yolk that spilled across the plate. "Your hopes and dreams."

"My hopes and dreams?"

"That's right."

The truth was, it had been a long time since she'd allowed herself to have hopes and dreams, but she didn't want to tell this stranger that. He already seemed to know too much about her.

"Well," she said, "when I was in high school, I used to dream about moving to Chicago or New York. I wanted to be a model."

Avery continued to work on his toast and eggs, dabbing his mouth with his napkin after each bite. "Really, a model? What happened?"

Tammi squirmed on the red Naugahyde bench. The little man's questions made her uncomfortable. She felt like an onion and each of his questions removed another layer of skin.

"I went to community college instead," she said. "I was going to learn computers, but . . ." Her voice trailed off.

Avery pushed his plate aside and sipped his coffee. He stared at her with those eyes. "Life's like that. But that was then, this is now. What are your hopes and dreams today?"

Tammi couldn't hold the man's gaze. In less than five minutes, he'd bought her attention with two hundred dollars, then dissected her like a frog on a table.

"I don't know. I'd go back to school to be a graphic artist, if I could."

"Graphic artist. Do you like to draw? Like to paint?"

"It's all done on computers these days."

"I didn't know that."

"So, what about you?" she asked. "You must have family."

"I'm just a man on the road."

"What about your hopes and dreams?"

He gave her a thin smile. What he said next caused her to sit back in her seat. "Would you be interested in modeling for me, Tammi?"

"Modeling?"

"Not tonight, but another time. Perhaps at the motel next door."

"The Sunrise?" She had a history with the Sunrise Motel. Dan had taken her there the night they graduated high school.

"Or some other place of your choosing."

"This is making me uncomfortable."

Avery's eyes never left hers. "I can change your life, Tammi."

She stood to leave. "Who says I need a change?"

He reached across the table and placed his hand over hers. "You should take the money."

The two $100 bills lay on the table. "I told you I didn't want your money."

"Take it, Tammi. For your trouble. No strings attached."

"You're crazy."

"Please. Take it."

Two rough-looking men pushed through the door. Shana had returned to the kitchen to refill her coffee pot.

"Y'all just sit anywhere," Tammi called to the men.

"Take the money, Tammi," Avery said.

She swallowed hard, scooped up the bills, and thrust them into her bra. She turned on her heel and strode away. She handed her new customers menus and poured them coffee.

When she looked back to where Avery had been sitting, he was gone. Cash paid his bill, and he left a twenty-percent tip.

Tammi sat on the toilet and smoked a cigarette. She removed the two crisp $100 bills from her bra. She sniffed them and held them to the light.

She didn't know what to make of it. People shouldn't go around paying other people good money to share their hopes and dreams. It wasn't right.

Then it occurred to her that she didn't have to keep the money. If Avery came back, she could return it. Or, she could give the money to Deac Williams, the Baptist preacher who always needed money for those starving kids in Africa.

Tammi stood, ground out her cigarette, and adjusted her skirt. She went out to finish her shift. By six, the sun was up on the prairie. The early-risers filled the diner with their raucous talk and laughter. By eight, the first rush was over and she headed home.

She could have returned the money or given it away, but instead, Tammi drove to the outlet mall and spent part of it on a new pantsuit from Bebe. With the rest, she bought some sexy new underwear from Victoria's Secret. It was her day off, so she had lunch at the Food Court, watched a movie in the afternoon, then ate dinner at the new Chinese restaurant they put up where the train station used to stand.

When she returned home, she stripped and showered. She made herself up, fixed her hair, and dressed in the new underwear and the tight-fitting pantsuit she'd bought earlier in the day. She liked the way the black thong snuggled between her butt cheeks. She liked the way the black bra lifted and separated her breasts.

She stood in front of the mirror. "Eat your fucking heart out, Dan," she said.

Since the divorce, she'd spent nearly every evening she wasn't working at home in front of the TV. But tonight, she looked too good to stay in. Tonight she was thinking she should call her friend Kate. That girl was always going on about the lounge at the bypass Holiday Inn. A lot of cute guys hung out there, Kate said. Some of them were even nice.

Tammi made several starts at calling Kate, but caught herself each time. Even in her new pantsuit, she worried about the extra pounds she'd put on and that new jiggle in her thighs. No one needed to see that. And those cute guys Kate talked about? Well, they were really traveling salesmen and losers on the make. If one of them picked her up, she'd be the chick he bragged about to all his buddies. *Yeah, you shoulda heard her moan like she hadn't been fucked in months.*

Okay, so she hadn't, but the whole world didn't need to know.

Worse yet, Kate had seen Dan there once, chatting it up with Pam Metzger, that floozy who tended bar at the Bowl-A-Matic. What would she say if she ran into Dan and one of his hotties? *Hi, Dan, I'm dating a great fella, but he didn't want to come out slumming with me tonight.*

The lounge at the Holiday Inn—who was she kidding?

Still dressed in her new clothes, Tammi went into the kitchen. She cut herself a piece of chocolate cake, loaded it up with Vanilla Bean ice cream, and carried it onto the front stoop of her mobile home.

It was high summer, hot and humid in Southern Illinois, even with the sun behind a bank of clouds. Air conditioners hummed loud enough to block the whine of the cicadas. Across the road, shoulder-high corn marched in rows as far as the eye could see. Now and then, a pickup truck chugged by.

Tammi ate until the cake and ice cream were gone. Then she licked the bowl.

Avery returned exactly one week to the day after he first showed his face at the diner. Tammi poured his coffee and took his order. Same gray suit, same pallid tie. Same eggs and toast.

This time, she didn't hesitate to sit when he asked.

He licked his lips with that same gray tongue.

"Tammi," he said.

"Avery."

She expected him to ask about the money he'd given her—if she'd spent it and how? But he didn't.

Instead, he reached inside his breast pocket and retrieved his wallet. He showed her another $100 bill, this one as crisp and clean as the first two he'd given her. "Have you thought anymore about what we talked about?"

"I thought about it."

"And?"

"Well, when you say modeling, what exactly . . ."

He cut her off. "I'd like your panties."

"My panties?"

"The ones you're wearing right now. I'd like you to go into the bathroom, take them off, then bring them to me. I'll pay you $100 for them."

"Last time . . ."

A dull light flickered in his eyes. "All right, $200, just like last time."

"But I thought you wanted me to model."

"Your panties," he said, his mouth full of eggs and toast.

Tammi told Shana she needed a bathroom break. She locked the door behind her, stepped into a stall, and lifted her skirt. She was wearing the black thong she'd bought with Avery's money. She stepped out of it and brought it to her face, inhaling the scent. She felt loose, almost giddy, when she walked back into the fluorescent light of the truck stop, naked underneath her waitress uniform.

She slid the rolled-up ball of fabric across the table and snatched up the little man's money.

He told her to lose ten pounds, do fifty sit-ups every day, and then they'd talk about modeling.

She bought some fancy running shoes and a set of twenty-pound dumbbells. She walked two miles every morning and every afternoon before going to work. She did belly crunches and lifted weights until her body glistened with sweat.

When Avery showed the next week, he complimented her. "You look good, Tammi," he said. "You've been working out."

"I gave up sweets too."

"Sweets aren't good for you."

Tammi fidgeted with a paper napkin. She could feel the little man's eyes on her. "No, they're not."

"I thought about you this week," he said. "I took your thong to bed with me each night."

Tammi blushed. She'd wondered about that thong, where it had been, what he'd done with it. "That's nice."

He sipped his black coffee, removed two $100 bills from his wallet, folded them, then folded them again. "I like your scent," he said, "the scent of your pussy."

The word caused Tammi to flinch. Shana was three tables away, serving Big Skillet Breakfasts to a sad-looking couple dressed in worn jeans and dirty T-shirts. The word seemed to fill the entire truck stop, yet Tammi couldn't stop herself from repeating it. "You like my pussy, Avery?"

"The scent of it. It excites you to say that word, doesn't it?"

"Maybe, a little. I guess."

When she glanced up, he was smiling. "I'm willing to bet your pussy is wet as we sit here."

She cleared her throat and placed her hands flat on the table. "You say the wildest things."

"Am I right?"

"Maybe, a little. I'm not used to talking about my pussy in public with strangers."

He slid the folded-up bills across the table. "Touch yourself under your dress. I want to smell you. I want to taste you."

THIRD SHIFT | 81

Tammi sat back. She felt hot and loose like she felt when she'd taken off her thong for him. "Here? Right now?"

He nodded and licked his lips. "No one's looking."

He was right about that. Shana had disappeared into the kitchen. The sad couple had their faces in their Big Skillet Breakfasts. Tammi bit her lower lip and slid a hand under her skirt. She pushed her panties aside and dipped two fingers inside her slick pussy. When she showed them to him, they glistened in the overhead light.

Avery brought her hand to his mouth. His tongue licked her fingers clean. His eyes burned a little brighter.

He placed the bills in her palm and folded her fingers around them. "I think you're almost ready," he said. "Write your phone number down for me."

He gave her a card with his name on it—AVERY SMITH—a white card with black print; it contained no further information. She wrote her number on the back as he'd instructed and returned it to him.

Then he told her to lose five more pounds.

After he left, she went into the bathroom and washed her hands. It didn't matter how many times she washed, she couldn't get the scent of her sex off. Then she realized the scent was emanating from between her legs. She couldn't remember the last time she'd been so worked up. Shit, she was on fire

Shana was waiting for her on the other side of the door. She was older than Tammi, divorced with two teenagers. She had a face like a horse and thick ankles.

"What the fuck are you up to?" Shana asked.

The truck stop had emptied out except for the two of them. "What do you mean?"

"That little man."

Tammi's mouth was dry. "Just talking. He's lonely."

"Every man comes in here's lonely. You take money from him?"

"No. Of course not. Why would he give me money?"

"You tell me, honey. I saw him hand you money."

Tammi felt the blood drain from her face. "He's harmless. Just a lonely little man."

Shana cocked an eyebrow. "There's a lot of weirdos in this world. Besides, if something funny's going on, it'll cost you your job."

"What do you mean, funny?"

"I think you know. There's only one reason that man would give you money."

Tammi frowned. "Well, who's going to say anything?"

"I've worked for Sam a long time. He won't put up with shit like that at The Dixie Highway."

"Well, nothing funny's going on."

"Whatever you say."

The next week, Avery called on her day off. He told her to meet him at midnight at the Sunrise Motel, Room 212. Tammi said okay and thanked her lucky stars it was a different room than the one where she'd spent graduation night with Dan. Avery said there was $500 in it for her.

After losing fifteen pounds and tightening her belly and thighs, she looked better than ever in her new pantsuit. She returned to the outlet mall and used more of Avery's money to buy an expensive pair of five-inch heels and a new black thong to replace the one she'd given him. At a CVS pharmacy on the other side of town, she purchased a pack of condoms from a pimply teenage boy. His arousal was palpable when she told him she wouldn't need a bag, and slipped the condoms into her purse.

In the shower that evening, she held a mirror with one hand while shaving her pussy bald as a bowling ball with the other. After shaving, she rubbed lotion into the sensitive flesh. The muscles in her thighs, buttocks, and calves rippled. When she tightened her belly, her abs stood out like rungs on a ladder. Her bare pussy looked strangely vulnerable, a dark line etched on white skin. She'd heard that men liked it, that little-girl look.

She was dressed and ready to go two hours before she needed to be. She sat on her porch stoop, smoking a cigarette and drinking a glass of box wine.

Avery answered her knock through the door and told her to let herself in. He sat in a straight-backed chair, wearing that same gray suit, neat and prim as ever.

His eyes traveled the length of her body. "You look like a whore."

Tammi felt like she'd been stabbed. "I thought . . ."

He shook his head. "Show me your breasts."

She removed her top and bra. Her breasts were smaller than before she'd lost the weight. They stood out firm and proud, her nipples stiff as pencil erasers.

"Can you suck them?" Avery asked.

"I don't know."

"Try."

For the first time, Tammi detected color in the little man's face. She craned her neck and stuck out her tongue. The tip barely grazed the nipple's end.

"Now, I want to see your pussy," he said. "Your pussy, your pussy, your pussy, Tammi." A bulge showed in his trousers and his left hand squeezed it absent-mindedly.

She wriggled out of the pantsuit and thong. She stood naked before him.

"You shaved."

"You like that, Avery?"

"I prefer it natural, actually. Turn around."

She spun in place, planted her feet wide apart, and thrust out her ass. She heard movement when Avery moved in for a closer look. She could feel his breath on her buttocks.

"Open your pussy lips for me," he whispered.

She spread herself using two fingers of her right hand.

"I can see your clitoris," he said. "Tammi's clit."

"It needs you, Avery." She couldn't believe she'd spoken the words.

Then she heard a muffled sob as he collapsed into the chair. She turned and looked down at him. He was breathing hard and a large wet stain showed on his pant leg. She reached out to touch him, but he waved her off.

He licked his lips, straining to regain his composure. "Your money's on the dresser," he said, nodding. "Next time, shop at Brooks Brothers and let your pussy hair grow back."

"That's it?" Tammi asked.

"I'll call you," he said. "You can get dressed now."

She threw on her clothes, took the five $100 bills, and fled to her car.

She woke up in her lounge chair, an empty wine box on the floor. On the Discovery Channel, some guy by the name of Bear was eating raw goat testicles with nomadic desert tribesmen. It had been one of Dan's favorite shows. She turned it off and made her way into the bedroom.

Still dressed in her new clothes, she stood in front of the mirror and struck one pose, then another. She thought about Avery and the money he'd given her. He wasn't there, but in a way, he was. The clothes belonged to him. Her new body belonged to him. Her soul even belonged to him. After all, she'd told him her hopes and dreams.

She struck another pose, her butt jutting toward where an imaginary Avery and his hundred-dollar bills sat in the chair. "You like that, Avery?"

Of course he did.

She unbuttoned her top and leaned over the chair. "You want these, Avery?"

Of course he did. His eyes widened. He licked his gray lips with his pale gray tongue.

Tammi stepped out of the pantsuit and swayed before Avery's chair. She unhooked her bra, and grasped the chair arms. She shook her breasts at the imaginary Avery.

"Oh yeah, you want 'em. Look at the big old boner in your pants, Avery."

She could almost see and smell him. She reached out and squeezed his pretend hard-on. For a little guy, he had a long, thick cock, more than enough to satisfy.

She held her left breast in her hand and milked it. She offered a nipple to Avery. "I'll let you suck it for $50."

The imaginary Avery licked and sucked her like a babe. "Fifty bucks for the other one," she said.

Old Avery obliged, just like she knew he would.

That's when she remembered the vibrating dildo Dan had bought not long before their divorce. He'd gotten off on fucking her with it. She hadn't enjoyed it all that much, but neither had she thrown it out. The dildo lay undisturbed in the drawer of her nightstand.

She placed it on the chair so it stood straight up.

"That's it, Avery, show me that big dick. I'll stroke it for $100."

Of course, he paid.

Tammi sank to her knees, wearing only the black thong. She held the dildo in her hand and stroked it up and down. It had been a while since she'd held a man's cock, but she hadn't forgotten how good it felt. And this felt like the real thing. It was veined and wrinkly. It had a dark ring and a thick ridge where the knife's blade had taken the extra flesh.

She spit into her hand, then spit again. "You like it, baby?" she asked, her voice husky, breathy.

She jacked him and pretended to watch his face. His eyes closed, his tongue flicked across those gray lips. "I'll suck it, if you want," she whispered, before taking the dildo in her mouth.

She'd never been all that excited about blow jobs. She'd never appreciated the way Dan placed his hand on top of her head and fucked her mouth like he was fucking the knothole of a tree. But this was different. She was giving Avery a blow job, not getting a mouth-fuck from Dan.

With her free hand, she rolled her nipples between her fingers. She reached lower and touched her pussy, pussy,

pussy through the fabric of her thong. My God, she was soaked through. She pushed the thong aside and worked a finger inside. She smeared her clit with girl-cum and rubbed.

"Shit," she heard herself say.

Tammi stood and stepped out of the thong. She rubbed the crotch in Avery's face. "Yeah, you like the way my pussy smells. You like the way it tastes, don't you? I'll fuck you for $500," she told the chair with the dildo on it.

Avery produced five Ben Franklins, pretty as you please.

Tammi turned around, facing away from the chair. She lowered herself onto the dildo. She used her thumb to rotate the on-off switch and felt the vibrations begin.

"Holy fuck."

She watched herself in the mirror. The sight of her swaying breasts, her thrusting hips, excited her even more.

"Goddamn sonofabitch."

She bounced in earnest.

"Fuck me, Avery," she said. "Come on, you paid for it, now fuck me good."

It was good. It was better than good. It was as hot and nasty as fucking the whole football team in the backseat of your daddy's Oldsmobile, which, of course, she never had.

She bounced harder and faster. She bounced until she felt it white-hot at her core. She wailed long and low, taking every inch of that dildo inside, grinding it out. Pulsing, pulsing, pulsing, she lavished in the aftershocks.

Then, she fell forward across the bed, breathing hard, her heart racing. "Jesus Christ," she said. "Jesus Fucking Christ."

She didn't even bother to wash her face, brush her teeth, or pee. She turned off the bedside light, slipped under the covers, and snuggled up with a pillow.

In the darkness, she imagined Avery hitching and zipping his pants. She imagined him opening his wallet and leaving a $100 tip on the nightstand.

The following week she drove to Springfield and shopped at the Brooks Brothers there. She bought a navy-blue business suit, a sharp-looking button-down cotton blouse, and black square-toed flats with a clunky brass buckle on them. She bought no-nonsense white cotton panties and a matching bra. She paired the bra and panties with flesh-colored pantyhose. By the weekend, her pubic hair reappeared as bristly whiskers that itched like crazy. By midweek, the whiskers transformed into a soft, dark fuzz, and the itch subsided.

While waiting for Avery's call, Tammi practiced opening and unrolling condoms onto her dildo. When she was able to do it expertly with one hand, she practiced applying the condoms using only her teeth and mouth. While she was at it, she worked on her deep-throat technique.

The call from Avery reached her at straight-up noon, the exact time of his first call. They arranged again to meet at the Sunrise, Room 212.

He was the same gray man he'd always been, but tonight he liked what he saw. She could tell by that dull flicker in his eyes.

He asked her to remove her pantyhose and open her legs, so he could look up her dress.

Then he asked her to jack him off onto her breasts. He lasted two minutes counting the time it took him to remove his suit. She used one hand to cup his balls while jacking him with the other. Her eyes never left his. When he was close, she pressed him between her breasts and held herself tight about him. He thrust and grunted and dribbled out a few drops. He paid her $500 and gave her a $100 tip, just like in her fantasy.

She was home in time to catch the 10:00 News.

Over the next few months, Tammi increased her fee to $1,000 plus tip, per session.

The third time they were together, he wanted her to masturbate for him. He propped pillows against the headboard and tweaked her nipples while she lay back against his chest and fingered herself so he could watch in the mirror opposite the bed. After she finished—a thrashing, gut-wrenching orgasm that surprised her as much as him—he asked for "oral."

She knelt on her knees while he sat on the edge of the bed and leaned back on his hands. She slipped on the condom without a hitch and sucked him slow and deep.

The following week, he asked to eat her pussy. Dan had never been into that, but Avery had the patience and persistence of a pro. His fingers and tongue took her from one orgasm to another, each one more powerful than the last. In the end, he sat across her chest and came on her face.

The week after that, he finally fucked her. She sat astride him, bouncing them both to a hard, quick come.

The next week, he took her from behind. He pulled her hair and slapped her ass. After he shot and rolled off, she lay beside him and humped his thigh until she got off. He stared at the ceiling, unmoving.

As summer turned to autumn, he wanted anal. She'd been ready for it and had practiced with her dildo. She accepted his tongue, his finger, his cock. When it was over, in a show of gratitude, he offered to eat her pussy again. She forced him onto his back, squatted over him, her bush now thick and redolent with her need. She ground against his face until she screamed it out.

The weeks acquired a rhythm. Sometimes, between their weekly sessions, he stopped into The Dixie Highway for coffee, toast, and eggs. Other times, he called after she got off work. With the muted TV flickering across the room, she talked him through it. She could be nasty or sweet, reluctant or demanding, whatever he wanted.

Sometimes when they were together, he just asked to hold her. She never stayed the night. He never acted like it was anything other than a business transaction.

Then, the week after Thanksgiving, as abruptly as he'd appeared in her life, he stopped calling. He stopped coming to The Dixie Highway for late-night breakfasts.

By then, their routine had begun to feel normal—as normal as coffee grounds in the sink at the end of her shift, as normal as piss on the men's room floor. By then, Tammi had already paid her first semester's tuition at the community college, signing up for classes in graphic art.

Along about Memorial Day, the last of Avery's money ran out. She'd used what was left over after paying tuition for a membership at the local health club and a closet full of Brooks Brothers' clothes. Her tips from The Dixie Highway wouldn't come close to paying her second semester's tuition.

One morning, just before sunrise, she and Shana stood smoking, looking out across the parking lot, Route 66, and onto the corn and soy beans pushing through the deep, black soil. The breakfast rush was only minutes off, but for now, it was quiet.

"That little man ain't ever coming back, is he?" Shana said.

"Probably not." Tammi had written him off with onset of the hot days.

"Well, hon, they come and go. He might've had a wife at home. He might've had other women on the road."

Tammi ground out her cigarette with the toe of her shoe. She'd considered both possibilities, but didn't want to believe either. "That's a mean-ass thing to say, Shana."

"I'm just calling it like I see it."

Tammi untied her apron, wadded it up, and fired it across the room. "Shana, you don't know shit," she said, striding out the door and across the parking lot.

Shana called out as Tammi was unlocking her car door. "Where you going? You can't leave me like this with the rush coming on."

"You'll be all right."

"You leave here now, you'll never be able to come back. I'll tell Sam. He'll never have you back."

"Tell him. I don't give a fuck."

Shana ran across the parking lot. Tammi settled behind the wheel and lowered the window. She figured she owed Shana that. After all, they'd worked together for ten years.

"What's going to happen to you, girl?" Shana asked.

"I don't know what's going to happen, but I know this—things aren't ever going to be the same."

It took her a few days to get her bearings. When she did, she set her sights on the Holiday Inn.

She strode into the lounge dressed in a gray pinstripe business suit and black silk blouse. Underneath, she wore black thigh-high stockings, black panties, and a tasteful black bra. Diamond earrings and a stylish gold necklace completed the sophisticated look. She settled on a barstool, lit a cigarette, and ordered a glass of red wine.

Smoke hung on the leaves of the fake ferns. A local DJ played music to the left of a deserted dance floor. The patrons, mostly single men, sat and drank alone. A few tired couples clung together in darkened corners, playing out secret trysts and the tiresome end of spent relationships.

It took only fifteen minutes for the first man to sit down beside her.

He was about her age, traveling alone in rumpled gray slacks, a navy sport coat, and a striped tie that hung loose about his neck. He'd had a little too much to drink and the ghost of his wedding ring, pale and white, showed where he'd removed it to his pocket before approaching her. He introduced himself as Joe Smith.

He offered to buy her a glass of wine. He told her he owned a successful business in St. Louis. He told her he was single and had never married, too committed to his work. He said he came this way often, on old Route 66, because he appreciated the "historical aspects of the journey." He said it was a rare and real pleasure to meet a woman like her—someone obviously smart, someone obviously able to take care of herself. Yeah, he liked strong, independent women.

She read it all for lies, like the lie of the missing wedding ring.

Finally, he asked her name and where she was from. He asked about her business and how much she traveled. He asked what she liked to do in her spare time, but stopped short of asking about her hopes and dreams. It was the typical salesman's ploy—get the prospect talking. Flatter her. Eventually, close her.

She told him her name was Shana, that she was a local, and self-employed. She told him she liked to work out, then she leaned in and whispered in his ear, "But what I really like to do is fuck."

He gave her a drunk and crooked smile. "Really?"

She placed her hand on his knee, the hand with the freshly manicured and painted nails. "Really."

"You like me that much?"

"I like you well enough."

His eyes narrowed to slits. "You're not a nut job, are you?"

She shook her head. "I'm not a nut job."

Then a wave of recognition washed over him. "You're a hooker."

She leaned in close again, whispering in his ear, "I'm just a woman who knows how to treat a man. My pussy's aching for you."

"You don't look like . . ."

She moved her hand a little higher. "For a thousand dollars, I'm anything you want me to be."

He mashed out his cigarette and took a deep breath. "A thousand bucks."

"There's an ATM in the lobby."

She slid off her stool and started for the door, putting a little extra into her walk for his benefit. Halfway there, she glanced over her shoulder.

Of course, he trailed behind as if he were on a leash.

Ray's Opening

My boyfriend Ray recently traveled to China for business. I drove him to LAX and kissed him good-bye at the security checkpoint. Afterwards, I cruised back to my place in Hermosa. The blue Pacific that would separate us for ten days broke in soft, warm waves along the beach. Surfers and volleyball players, lean, strong, and tan, exulted in their skills. I pouted and resigned myself to dining in front of the TV, reading alone on my deck, and satisfying my carnal urges with my own hand until he returned.

I began fantasizing about Ray's opening almost from the moment of his departure.

I was thirty-four and Ray was forty-two. I was a lawyer, paid to defend thieves, murderers, and drug-pushers. He was an aeronautics engineer, paid to design and build telecommunication satellites. I called him my Rocket Scientist. He called me his Shyster Bitch. We were bound together, not so much by oral commitments of love and monogamy as by an irrepressible attraction to the intricacies of the other's mind and a profound need for the other's body.

I admit my body was not quite the same as when I was a law student in New Orleans—pole-dancing and working as a line cook to pay my tuition bills. Yet, I strove to maintain mystery in my brown eyes and wickedness in my smile. My legs remained long and lean from running and I kept my tummy and tush firm with Pilates. My breasts were never that large, anyway, so gravity's pull had little adverse effect.

For his part, Ray was one of those tall, lanky guys with salt-and-pepper hair and fur all over his body. His balls hung low and swung delightfully when he walked. His cock was long and thick and never failed to rise to the occasion. He hadn't exercised a day in his life, yet sported abs to die for and the roundest, tightest, most boyish butt I'd ever seen on a man. He was a walking, talking Calvin Klein ad.

On the surface, we were total nerds. He preferred *Popular Mechanics* to drinking beer with the guys, while I favored a cooking class over shopping with the girls. But scratch the surface and we were devoted sensualists. My sister called us artsy-fartsy, which was quite a compliment for a lawyer and an engineer.

There wasn't much we hadn't tried. In the year and a half we had been together, we'd bent and stretched into every position we could safely assume. We buzzed and plied my orifices with a closet-full of vibrators and toys. We fucked in public bathrooms and I blew him on the beach. He fingered me under the table at Spago and I stroked him off onto a tablecloth at Josie in Santa Monica. We tied each other up and one spanked until the other cried out.

But the one thing we hadn't explored was Ray's opening.

The following evening, he called, sounding jet-lagged and disoriented. The time difference placed him outside a meeting room on his international cell phone and me between the sheets of my bed. I'd stripped naked except for a black thong and was hoping for at least a phone sex dalliance.

Alas, it was not to be.

First, he wasn't exactly in the mood, having just stepped out of a conference where US rocket scientists shared circuit board technology with Chinese scientists for big bucks. Even Ray couldn't make an unfettered transition from the nuances of nanophysics to sucking my pussy over the miles.

Second, he reminded me that phone calls and e-mails in China were subject to government scrutiny and arrests of foreign visitors for engaging in sexual behavior were not uncommon. Sex blogs, dirty chat rooms, and porn video downloads were criminal activities in the People's Republic.

So, after a brief conversation of the plain vanilla variety, Ray rang off and I was left, literally, to my own devices.

I turned to my first full-blown fantasy of Ray's opening and a little silver bullet that had served me well over the years.

I couldn't say where this sudden fascination with the man's butt-hole had originated. I characterized myself as neither a Nazi fem-domme, who got off on bossing around boys, nor a groveling submissive, who doted on her lover's every whim, because I had taken pleasure from both sides of the equation. For me, it depended on the person I was with and the situation.

For example, there was this older, red-haired woman I knew in New Orleans years ago. I played the role of her slave for several months. Allowing someone else to set limits and make decisions appealed to me at that time. Besides, she often topped from the bottom and I took pleasure from diddling her with a large black dildo we kept for such events.

Fuck me, Alicia. Fuck me with your big cock.

Take it, baby. Take it.

On the other hand, to pay the bills while in law school and for an impoverished time thereafter, I also worked as a phone-sex goddess. An often-requested fantasy was for me to dominate my caller. I was surprised to learn that powerful, highly paid men actually got hard pretending to be *my* slave and satisfying *me* while denying their own gratification until I chose to allow it. With a creative, intelligent, and articulate guy on the other end of the line, it could be quite a turn-on.

Please, Alicia, I need to come.

Not yet. Lick my clit for a while longer, bee-atch.

But I didn't attribute my sudden fascination with Ray's opening to a repressed need to dominate or defile him. Instead, I saw it as achieving equality in our relationship.

I mean, if he could penetrate me, if he could fuck me, why couldn't I penetrate him? Like my grandmother used to say— what's good for the goose is good for the gander.

So, that night, after hanging up the phone, I considered Ray's opening in earnest. I pressed my little silver bullet against the fabric of my thong and allowed it to do its magic while my mind did its own thing. I fantasized about going down, way down, on Ray. I thought about opening his opening. I imagined the expression on his face. I pictured his knees pulled up to his chest, his cock and balls mercilessly exposed.

I pushed the fabric of my thong aside and touched my clit with the bullet. I circled and probed as images of Ray's pucker formed behind my closed eyes. His cock throbbed and spurted, and I came in a twisting, thrashing, groaning rush.

I came, so to speak, on Ray's opening.

Over the next few days, I focused on work. I was in the midst of jury selection in the trial of my client, Noreen Winchell. You may remember her as the Beverly Hills Blaster Babe—as the press dubbed her after she was arrested for emptying her 9mm Beretta into her husband at point-blank range. When I asked why she did it, she told me that a better question was why she'd waited so long.

She and Wayne had been married for over forty years and although he had become a famous film director, he was mostly a domestic abuser. It was the kind of case every defense attorney hungers for—a well-heeled client who can afford to pay big bucks and free advertising through out-of-control press coverage.

I opted for a battered-woman defense as an alibi was out of the question.

Yet, while *voir dire* dragged on and Noreen bit her nails at the defense table next to me, my mind wandered. I was more interested in devising a strategy for obtaining entry to Ray's opening than in selecting jurors sympathetic to my client. Even though she'd killed her husband while he slept for something he hadn't done that night, the jury had to believe she shot him for the accumulated kicks, slaps, and verbal denigrations she'd endured over the years.

Older males were out and aging hippie-chicks were definitely in. So, while the assistant DA, Mort Cone—a fellow I'd been up against in several other trials—questioned potential jurors, I concluded that the way to Ray's opening was through Alicia's opening.

For me, almost nothing was as pleasurable as having my asshole tongued while my pussy was fingered. And I pretty much made this a prerequisite to anal sex. Quite simply, if a man wanted to put his dick inside my dark hole, he needed to lick me there first.

Unfortunately, not all men were up to the task. I've been with a few who were too tentative, who seemed repulsed, or who appeared to do it solely for my pleasure. I preferred a man who was confident in his efforts, who loved my taste and smell, and who enjoyed eating me as much as fucking me.

In my experience, chefs ate pussy and licked ass better than anyone. I attributed their collective skills to a heightened sensitivity to flavor and aroma. When I worked as a line cook, the chef was a fat Cajun with a passion for my menu. On the nights when I didn't go to my second job as a pole dancer, Robert and I would stay after everyone had gone home. I'd sit on the edge of one of the gleaming stainless steel tables we used for food prep and he'd kneel on the floor. I'd lift my skirt over my hips, spread my legs, and he'd dine on me forever.

But the best times were when he'd position me against the door of the big, walk-in pantry. I'd lean into it, hike up my skirt, and he'd burrow into me from behind. It's one thing to look down and see a man's hair, forehead, and eyes looking up from between your thighs while he diligently plies your nether regions, but it's another sensation entirely when a man eats you from behind. Part of it is that the angle is different. Part of it is that if he's doing a good job on your pussy, really going after it, his nose is inevitably buried in your asshole. There's no getting around it. And if he's a real man, once his nose is there, he won't flinch at visiting your backdoor with his tongue and lips. Robert was such a man and he'd have me screaming and gyrating against his face in no time.

Finally, it was my turn with the jury panel. I crossed the room, my Manolo Blahniks clicking, my Neiman Marcus pinstriped skirt rustling, and began my questioning. I used my preemptory challenges to exclude two older white men, a couple of young Hispanics, and a fundamentalist Christian who told me she thought it was proper for a husband to strike his wife if she disobeyed. On the flip side, I selected two baby-boomers, one dressed for jury duty in a tie-dyed T-shirt and the other wearing a peace symbol necklace circa 1969.

I'm pretty sure no one in the courtroom—including a very astute Superior Court judge by the name of Seamus Moody—was aware that Noreen Winchell's able lawyer, namely me, was addressing the court with damp satin panties. The thought of my upcoming enjoyments with Ray had my pussy oozing nectar like an overripe fruit.

In his absence, Ray and I continued to communicate by phone. As I said, the Chinese government made intimacy difficult, but I devised clever ways to hint at what he could expect when he returned.

In one phone conversation, where he described the joys of authentic Chinese cuisine, I interrupted to say that my personal hotpot had been empty of late and that I required a sturdy bamboo shoot to fill it. I could hear Ray's breathing quicken all the way from China.

Just as cleverly, he reported the recent discovery of an especially sturdy variety of bamboo. Most interestingly, when inserted into a steamy hotpot and stirred, this bamboo would eventually issue a frothy, white liquid.

"Can the liquid be obtained by stroking or sucking the shoot?" I inquired.

He said it could, particularly if the stroker or sucker knew her business and was diligent in her efforts.

I told him that if he listened carefully, he could hear my hotpot boiling.

I slid a hand past my belly and fingered myself lightly with one hand while holding the phone with the other. The squishy sounds of my masturbation filled the room and coursed across the sea.

"If you were here, you could stir my pot with your shoot," I suggested.

"I have a firm grip on my shoot as we speak."

"Next to my boiling hotpot," I whispered seductively, "is a chocolate pot."

"A chocolate pot?"

"Do they have chocolate in China?"

"Based on what I've seen, the Chinese have chocolate pots too. Some of the Chinese maidens carry them well."

"Would your bamboo shoot issue its liquid if inserted in my chocolate pot?"

"God, yes."

"Yes," I murmured, "my chocolate pot needs a good stir. Maybe the electric blender will work."

I flipped the switch on a slender vibrator we'd purchased at a boutique in West Hollywood and inserted the tip of the vibe into my opening.

"You are certainly giving your chocolate pot a good stir," Ray said breathily, and I knew he was stroking himself.

"As it turns out," I replied, "my hotpot needs attention while my chocolate pot is stirred."

"I'm your huckleberry," Ray intoned.

"Put your bamboo shoot inside my chocolate pot. I'll stir my hotpot myself."

"Your chocolate pot is quite tight. I mean, small," Ray said, his voice husky.

"It's just that your bamboo shoot is so big. It's all my chocolate pot can handle."

"My bamboo shoot is about to melt," he said.

"My hotpot is about boil over," I managed.

"Now?"

"Yes, now. Now, now, now."

"Oh, Alicia."

"Oh, Ray."

"My bamboo shoot exploded on my belly," he confessed.

"Is it messy?"

"Yes, very."

"If I were there, I would lick up every drop. I'm sure it's tasty."

"I should probably fetch a towel."

I set the vibe aside while continuing to caress my clit. "Stay with me," I implored him, "I think my hotpot may boil over again."

And it did. Twice more.

"May it please the court . . ."

The day of Ray's return also marked the beginning of Noreen Winchell's trial. Festivities kicked off with Mort Cone's tedious monotone. For two long hours, he bored the jurors, the judge, and the press with his opening statement. The prosecution would show that the defendant had the means, motive, and opportunity. Blah, blah, blah. In conclusion, etc.

After a short recess, it was my turn. I'd selected a plain black suit, an inexpensive cotton blouse, and a pair of square-toed heels purchased from TJ Maxx for the occasion, eschewing high fashion in favor of the common touch. Underneath, I wore a camisole in lieu of a bra and nude thigh-highs *sans* panties in anticipation of my rendezvous with Ray later on.

These jurors wanted to do a good job, but like the rest of us, they had their own lives to live. As much as they cared about Noreen Winchell's guilt or innocence, they were distracted by the memory of an argument with a spouse, the humiliation of being cut off in traffic, or perhaps the need to pee. Who knows?

My job was to engage them in the task at hand.

My eyes searched from one to the other. I leaned across the rail that separated us and gave one of the male jurors a glimpse of cleavage.

"We do not dispute that Mrs. Winchell shot her husband on the night of June fourth," I began. "However, the evidence will show that she did so out of fear and pent-up rage, not a premeditated intent for murder. She did so to end her suffering at her husband's hand, not for monetary gain or the desire to take another lover. Who among us has not felt fear and rage? Who among us has not been pushed nearly to the edge?"

Here, I paused, knowing that Noreen's life hung in the balance. I released the rail and paced before the jurors' box. I put a little extra into my sway, thinking that the men would like it and the women would understand.

I turned dramatically and began anew.

"My client is neither a monster nor a cold-blooded murderess. Indeed, she is you and me. The only difference is that she reached the precipice and leapt, while we, so far, have held our ground."

The jurors leaned forward. The one who was taking notes paused in her efforts and simply listened. Juror Number Three, a wispy-haired man with a wispier mustache, stroked his chin and eyed me as if I were a morsel of chocolate.

"If you believe this, then you must find Noreen Winchell innocent of murder as charged. If you believe this, then you must allow her punishment to be her own remorse and not a gas chamber's stench. If you believe this, you must find her not guilty."

The mostly female jury nodded in agreement. I had them eating from my hand.

For the next hour and a half, I described 911 calls made by Noreen over the years, showed photos of the injuries she'd endured, and read an e-mail from Noreen to her sister that detailed her fear and suffering. By the time I concluded, I was confident I'd won the first round.

On the way back to my place next to Noreen, I winked at Mort. As I assumed my seat, I crossed my legs, giving Judge Moody a glimpse of the good stuff. It never hurts to have the judge think well of you during a difficult trial. I sighed. The exacting examination of witnesses lay before us.

Now, if I could only get through the rest of the day.

I saw him as he came through the door from Customs into Baggage Claim. The Eternal Nerd, he wore a goofy grin, a white polo shirt, jeans, and a wrinkled blue blazer. He strode toward me with that gangly walk he probably acquired in high school Electronics Club. He was unshaven and smelled like the inside of an airplane. We kissed and it was like coming home on Christmas vacation. He held me while we waited for his bags and I clung to him like a groupie with a rock star.

"I missed you," he conceded.

"I missed you too." I stood on my toes and nibbled his earlobe. Then, I gave him a sniff of my fingers. I'd been touching myself the entire trip down Sepulveda Boulevard. I'd even inserted a forefinger into my opening just before leaving the garage.

"You are such a wicked woman," he said.

"Yes, I am."

I stepped into him the moment we closed the door to my place. Our tongues darted like feral animals. I backed him up against the wall opposite my bookshelf—on which, law books competed for space with Bobby Ann Mason and Zadie Smith—and unbuttoned his shirt. His hands slid down my back and over the curve of my hips.

"Shyster Bitch," he gasped, his breath hot on my ears and neck.

"Rocket Scientist," I whispered into the mat of hair across his chest.

My dress fell to the floor. Naked except for my camisole and thigh-highs, I ran my fingers through his hair. He caressed my buttocks. Blood pounded in my temples.

Suddenly, he spun us around, pressed me to the wall, and wedged a knee between my thighs. I ground my pelvis against him.

He lifted the camisole over my head. My breasts spilled into his waiting hands. I bit my lower lip and we locked eyes while he squeezed. He lowered his mouth to my nipples, gracing first one, then the other, with his tongue.

"Oh, baby," I heard myself say.

I loosened his belt buckle and reached inside. I needed to feel his hardness in my hand, its throb and ache. I reached lower and cupped his balls in my palm.

He backed away and shucked his jeans and shorts. He pulled me after him onto the sofa where I straddled his belly.

He looked up, his face red, his breath short. "I want you."

"Yeah, you want these?" I leaned forward, brushing my nipples against his, teasing him.

"Oh, yes."

He reached for my breasts, but I guided him to between my legs. "You want this?"

"Fuck yes."

His fingers opened me, drawing moisture. His eyes never leaving mine, he fingered me until I cried out.

I rose up on my haunches, positioned the tip of his cock, and sank onto him. I felt him enter me, fill me, stretch me. I sighed and heard him do the same.

I began to rock. He sucked at my purple nipples. He ran his hands over my torso. When his fingers trailed lightly down to the crease of my ass, I rocked faster.

My orgasm hit before his. It ignited deep inside my cunt, pulsed outward, cascaded up through my breasts, and seized my throat like a prowler in the night.

When I collapsed, he held me for a moment, bathing my face and forehead with butterfly kisses. He began to pump in and out, the muscles in his hips and abdomen bouncing us both on the sofa. When I reached behind and squeezed his sack, I felt his balls rise. Then, I felt his warmth gush inside my warmth.

"Damn," he whispered.

"You can say that again."

"Damn."

It's always good to get that first one out of the way.

Later, after we'd indulged in a long, languid bath and a bottle of Chardonnay, I lay on my belly, legs wide apart. Ray's tongue searched my opening. He rimmed the wrinkles on the outside, then mined deeper. I encouraged his efforts, secure in my knowledge that the way to Ray's opening was through Alicia's opening.

After driving me to the edge, he reached for the lube. No doubt he'd earned a good ass-fuck, but this night, I had other things in mind.

I sat up, pushed Ray onto his back, set the lube aside, and said, "Not so fast, Rocky."

He looked at me with wonder and trepidation. We were about to make history.

Not every woman is up for eating her man's asshole. Not every man is ready for it. Not every relationship can stand it. In my experience, few men will ask, but hardly any will refuse. There are more nerve endings in the anus than in the penis. There is something forbidden and downright nasty about going for a man's opening.

And after obsessing about it for a couple of weeks, I wanted Ray's opening in the worst way. I wanted to make him scream. I wanted to make him my bitch.

I began with a little head.

I'm not talking a mere blow job—anyone can bob off a blow job. I'm talking about making love to his cock and balls. I'm talking about looking up at him with his cock in my mouth, letting my eyes ask him how he likes it. I'm talking about making a pussy of my hand and lips and stroking him between them. I'm talking about rolling his balls inside my mouth until he can't stand it, grabs for his cock, and starts to jerk off.

I'm talking about kissing my way down to his opening.

Ray groaned and lifted his hips. I tasted him, earthy and raw. I swirled around the outside and flicked at the middle. He groaned again. He thrashed about. He called my name.

We repositioned and I lay on my back. He squatted above me while my tongue darted and delved. The window to our bedroom was open and we were not far from the beach. Above the rising crescendo of his moans, I could make out the crashing of waves, the cries of gulls, and the murmur of people passing not ten feet away. I parted my pussy, inviting his view, aware that I was pink and shiny with girl-cum. It was *Alicia, Alicia, Alicia,* and I knew I had him. I knew from the hastened *slap, slap* of his hand on his cock and the quickened pucker of his opening.

But I wanted more. I wanted to make him my bitch.

I stretched him out and pinned his arms to the bed. Then I reached inside the drawer of our nightstand. The strap-on dildo was life-size and life-like, an exact replica of some sweet man's erect member, complete with veins and ridges. Ray's eyes were ablaze with fear and anticipation.

I sat on his chest and fed it to him, stuffing my girl-cock into his mouth. He surprised me, making little sucking noises as I slid in and out. The dildo served as an extension of my clit. Each flick of the silicon tweaked flesh already raw with want. I would've given anything to spray a load down his throat, across his lips and cheeks.

I withdrew and applied lube to my finger, then his opening.

"Do you want it?" I asked. My finger danced like a gypsy at the door.

"Yes," he exhaled, quick and sharp.

I pushed and he withdrew.

"Relax, baby. Do you want it?"

"Yes," he squeaked.

I pushed harder and felt his muscle accept my singular probing digit. Oh, he was tight.

Beyond our window, revelers lit a fire on the beach. There were shouts and laughter. In our bed, I held my lover in my hand. I pumped in and out. He looked dazed, transported to an arena of lust that knew no boundary and had only one exit.

Next, I applied lube to the cock.

He pulled his knees to his chest. His tight, brown opening winked at me, his hard cock throbbed. I positioned myself and eased the dildo's tip inside. When I pushed farther, he bellowed like a wounded bull.

And then I fucked him. His mouth opened in an "O" and the whites of his eyes showed in the slits. I fucked him hard and true like a bitch should be fucked.

He couldn't take it for long and neither could I. Each advance of the dildo was an assault on my clit, still sensitive from the ghost of his tongue. I sank hilt-deep into Ray's opening and reached for him. I gave his cock a squeeze and his expression changed from rapture to gratitude. This man needed to come and I wanted to watch. I wanted to feel it on my hands, wanted to rub it on my tits and face, wanted to eat it like candy.

I delivered him with a couple of short strokes. Still impaled on my cock, he squirted strings into the air, moaning and mewing like a backseat virgin. He floated in his own space while I bucked my way to a torso-twisting climax. Cum-soaked and sated, I disintegrated onto Ray's bare chest.

Noreen Winchell's trial plodded on. Mort Cone competently presented the prosecution's case, beginning with the neighbor who called in the gunshots, continuing with the cute young patrolman who first responded, and concluding with a crusty detective and an array of geeky criminologists. It lasted for three long weeks.

My cross-examination focused on the detective's ineptitude. No, he hadn't examined Noreen for bruises. No, he hadn't asked if she'd been assaulted by her deceased husband that evening. No, he hadn't bothered to research the many calls Noreen had made over the years reporting her husband's degradation of her. Yes, the LAPD rewarded him for making arrests and clearing cases. Yes, he'd been disciplined in the past for planting evidence to justify an arrest. Yes, he'd written Noreen's confession and asked her to sign it, rather than audio or video-taping it, and accordingly, it was possible he had embellished or summarized her words.

Our best witness was the psychotherapist, Dr. Werner Faust, who we retained to evaluate Noreen's state of mind. Equipped with more advanced degrees than a tenured USC professor, he testified that the rage that had been building inside her for years bubbled forth the night of the murder. She killed, not in cold blood, but in hot blood, notwithstanding the fact that her husband had not touched her that particular evening. He explained how women are different from men in this respect.

No shit, Sherlock!

Under Cone-Head's less than withering cross-examination, Faust held strong. He refused to agree with Cone's point that, even if Noreen had been abused over the years, it was possible she'd acted with premeditated intent to kill that fateful night.

By the time our case concluded, I expected an outright acquittal or, at worst, a conviction for voluntary manslaughter with probation instead of jail time.

I couldn't have been more wrong.

What I hadn't anticipated, because Noreen had neglected to mention it, was that she and Wayne were BDSM devotees, according to the testimony of several witnesses Cone introduced on redirect. The bruises and abrasions for which she'd received medical treatment over the years had been received consensually in sessions at a local club where Wayne spanked and whipped his wife for their mutual pleasure and that of other attendees. Even more damning was the revelation that Wayne had recently jilted Noreen in favor of a porn-star who starred in one of his movies, a Mistress Jade Landrieu. The inference being that Noreen killed her husband not out of pent-up rage, but out of ordinary jealousy.

Despite my efforts to rehabilitate Noreen and to shed doubt on the prosecution's case, the jury's decision was swift and to the point.

Noreen was found guilty, but received life in prison rather than the death penalty.

It was the beginning of the end of my career as a defense attorney. Noreen jettisoned me in favor of a predatory barrister from downtown LA who based his appeal on my incompetence at trial. I could offer little rebuttal to his claim that I'd been distracted during the trial and failed to conduct a complete investigation.

What this shark didn't know was that the cause of my negligence was, no doubt, my obsession with Ray's opening. Rebuked by the local Bar Association and the subject of reams of negative publicity, I adopted a bunker mentality. Clients stopped calling, cash-flow dried up, and I was forced into a second career.

I moved to Napa, opened a restaurant, and have recently found a spiritual connection with the soil.

As for Ray and I, the opening of his opening was also the beginning of the end.

Instead of the smart, virile, take-charge man I'd come to know and love, Ray became an insufferable sycophant and a mewly do-gooder. He agreed without me badgering him to attend romantic films, took an interest in chick-lit authors such as Helen Fielding and Plum Sykes, and switched from plain white jockey shorts to fly-less microfiber undies in assorted pastels. He picked up after himself, remembered to change the toilet paper, and required more foreplay than is normal for a man.

I had emasculated my poor baby.

After I left for Napa, I learned through mutual friends that he quit his job as a high-powered rocket scientist to work instead with inner-city youth and reconsidered his sexual orientation.

Then he moved in with another man.

I still think about Ray's opening from time to time, usually when we're prepping chocolate *crème brûlée* or I'm dining on Chinese. But, so far, I've resisted the path of least resistance. My new lover is a delicately featured, talented, and strong-willed *sous* chef fresh from the Culinary Institute. He has sensitive brown eyes, sensual lips, and a rump as hard as an autumn apple. He has exquisite taste and tastes me exquisitely.

Knowing that the path to his opening is through my opening, and given my experience with Ray, I've made my opening off limits.

So far.

SAVAGE NIGHTS

"Stop," Bobby said.

"I'm not doing a thing."

We were in his 1965 Mustang in the lot across from the high school where we'd graduated two days earlier—Dunlap High, Class of '67. Christiana Creek bubbled nearby and a breeze rattled the corn on the other side of the creek.

I snuggled and nibbled his earlobe.

"You know that drives me crazy," he said.

My blouse was open. His class ring dangled on a chain between my bare breasts.

I turned and slid into the backseat. "Come on, if you want to go again."

"Shit, you know I do."

"Here." I spread a blanket across the seat. "We don't want to ruin the leather."

He helped me out of my jeans for the second time that night. "It's not leather. It's Naugahyde. Anyway, I don't give a damn."

He wriggled out of his jockey shorts. I lay down, an armrest across the small of my back, and opened my legs.

"Yeah, but I do, and that's the difference between us."

He kissed me, his tongue swirling inside my mouth. He tasted of beer and cigarettes, and the cheeseburger he'd eaten at Ozzie's Drive-In two hours earlier. "There ain't no difference between us."

I reached below his flat belly, grasped his hard cock, and guided him to my opening. I was wet and musky as a field of mushrooms. "I just meant . . ."

"It don't matter. This is all that matters."

He thrust and I lifted my hips to greet him.

The car rocked. Over his shoulder, the rear window steamed. I felt a quickening between my thighs. Then no sooner had it begun than it was over. He exploded into me, his heat in mine.

"I love you, Bobby," I whispered.

"I love you too, Trish."

Even then, I knew—it wasn't a lie, but it wasn't exactly the truth, either, because neither of us had a clue what it meant.

Three weeks later, Bobby enlisted in the Army. Never mind that there was a war raging in Vietnam and they were shipping boys home in body bags by the thousands. Never mind that the war was lost and even the President knew it.

I said, "Bobby, have you lost your fucking mind?"

He said, "It's a tough job, but someone has to do it."

I said, "Yeah, but that don't mean you."

His best friend Mike begged him not to go. "Make love, not war, man." But that was easy for Mike to say. He had a student deferment from the draft and a scholarship to Ball State. You know, Testicle Tech, Blue Ball U.

That was his ticket out of Dunlap.

Anyway, Bobby's mind was made up. Now I understood why he hadn't cared if we'd ruined the backseat of his Mustang. He'd planned to sell it all along when he shipped out.

A few days following his big announcement, Bobby gave me a line about needing to get his head together before going off to shoot people. He quit his job and he and Mike loaded the trunk of Mike's Chevy Nova with beer. They set off to find America in Bobby's last three weeks of civilian life.

They didn't ask if I'd like to go.

When Bobby waved good-bye, I raised my middle finger and held it high until the Nova was out of sight.

That evening, I pedaled my bike to our make-out spot. I sat on the creek bank, smoking Virginia Slims. I swatted mosquitoes and grabbed for fireflies.

Music played on my transistor radio. Jefferson Airplane sang "Somebody to Love." The Beatles did "Penny Lane." Then this chick Bobbie Gentry started crooning about some guy named Billie Joe jumping off the Tallahatchie Bridge. That song made me so sad I started to cry.

After I got it out, I wasn't sad anymore—just hurt and pissed. I ripped Bobby's class ring from my neck and threw it into the creek.

I didn't want the damn thing, and he sure as hell wouldn't need it where he was going.

That summer, I lived at home and waitressed at The Checkerboard Tap. Because I worked days and my mom worked nights, we hardly saw each other. It wasn't a bad thing. She hadn't been the same since my dad lost his job at

Studebaker and struck out for parts unknown. When she wasn't working, she was sleeping or hanging out at the bars with her best friend Noreen.

I didn't have the heart to tell them how ridiculous they looked—hair in beehives, dressed up like Nancy Sinatra in miniskirts and boots.

We lived in Sunnyside Estates. A train track ran beside our subdivision and separated us from The Shady Acres Trailer Park across the way. Thing was, there wasn't a tree standing in Shady Acres or anything stately about Sunnyside—just row after row of boxy little houses.

Trains ran all night. I'd sit on the porch, smoke cigarettes, and listen to their long, low whistles.

I could have called my friends, Nancy or Rhonda, but that meant having to explain about Bobby and me. That meant having to explain about his class ring. Besides, since graduation, it wasn't the same. Like a nine-ball rack exploded by a break shot, we'd gone our separate ways. The Class of '67 had begun its solitary trek into adulthood.

So, I smoked and listened to trains.

Until our new neighbors moved in.

I met Wendy Goldfinger a few days after Bobby and Mike left town. She arrived at the rental next door in a Volkswagen minibus. The bus was painted psychedelic colors with flowers and sunbursts. She wore an ankle-length skirt. Up top, braless breasts swam beneath a tie-dyed T-shirt. A bouquet of daisies was tucked into the headband that captured her long blonde hair.

No sooner had Wendy's sandals hit the ground than one young man climbed out the rear of the bus and another came around from the passenger's side. Buck was tall and dark. Thick fur showed beneath his leather vest. Curly hair fell to his shoulders and black eyes flashed behind a Jesus beard. Jude, the other guy, was tan and muscular with sea-blue eyes and a surfer's smile.

Wendy strode across the yard and unlocked the door to their new house. The men started unloading their stuff. I lit another cigarette and pretended not to watch. After a few minutes, Wendy reappeared.

"Shitter works," she announced.

Then she placed her hands on her hips and looked around. When her eyes fell on me, she called out, "Hey, sweetie, you got any weed?"

"See," Wendy said through a purple haze, "the universe is like wheels inside of wheels, like one of those Russian babushka dolls, dolls inside of dolls. The wheels turn, the dolls shrink. We're all connected. It goes on and fucking on."

"Heavy," Buck said. He sat next to her on their yard-sale loveseat that smelled of Indian curry and cat piss.

Jude reached out, removed the roach from Buck's fingers, took a deep drag, then passed it to me.

I'd never tried weed before, but I liked the way it made me feel. The room glowed pink and soft. I floated in the haze.

"I never thought of it like that," I told Wendy.

"It's all about opening your mind and letting the sun shine in."

She was twenty-four, an artisan, a creator of silver and gold ornaments. Buck had completed two tours of duty in "The Nam," as he called it, but was now dedicated to bringing the war to an end. Jude was Buck's cousin, a couple of years older than me. He played guitar and wrote music. They were on their way from New York to San Francisco.

"Wheels," Jude said to no one in particular. "That's so far out."

Wendy lit incense and candles. She sifted through a stack of records, selected The Doors, and fit the album onto the turntable. She began to dance to those first hard driving chords of "Break on Through." She spun and tripped through the room. She raised her skirt over her knees, revealing strong thighs. Beneath the thin top, her breasts rolled. There were no steps to this dance, just joy on the move.

She curled a finger at me. "C'mon, sweetie, shake that thing."

Reluctantly, I rose to my feet and began to dance. I wore short, tight cut-offs and a T-shirt. I felt the unexpected heat of Buck and Jude's eyes on me.

I knew the men who came to The Checkerboard saw something in me they liked. I'd overheard them admiring my ass and legs. They said I had boobs to die for. Bobby had wanted me, of course, but that was just Bobby—I'd known him since third grade. It came as a surprise that anyone else would want me. I still thought of myself as a skinny brunette with pimples and glasses.

But here I was, shaking it, teasing these men like a gypsy in the firelight. It made me feel powerful and womanly in a way I'd never felt before.

When we reached "The End," Wendy crashed onto Buck's lap. I continued dancing and it took me a moment to realize they were kissing. Then he had her top off and a hand up her skirt. She touched him through his jeans.

I felt Jude's hand on my elbow.

"C'mon," he said.

We walked outside and leaned against the minibus. He lit a Winston and I lit another Virginia Slim.

"They get a little carried away," he said.

"Hey, I'm cool."

Not as cool as I pretended to be.

"Yeah, but they hardly know you."

Far above, waves of multi-colored light rolled across the sky. "Look," I said.

"What is it?"

"The Northern Lights. We get them every summer."

He rummaged inside the minibus, found a blanket, and spread it on the ground. We lay on our backs, taking in the incredible display. He talked about growing up in New Jersey, about swimming at The Shore, about trips into The City. He said he'd played gigs in The Village and even met Bob Dylan and Joan Baez there.

I half-believed him.

I talked about growing up in crummy, little Dunlap. I explained about Bobby and me. A train passed on the tracks, not thirty yards away. Over the clanking of metal on metal, I said I'd give anything to get out of this place.

"Come to San Francisco," he said. "Wear some flowers in your hair."

"San Francisco?" It was too far away to imagine.

"Sure? Why not? Besides, I gotta go somewhere."

He confided that he was on the run after burning his draft card and failing to show up for his physical.

"If enough of us say no, we'll bring the military-industrial complex to its knees," he told me.

"What if they catch you?"

"They won't catch me."

He rolled, stretched his body over mine, and worked a knee between my legs. He pushed my hair out of my face. "Come to The Haight. We'll get high every night, make love every day."

"I don't . . ."

He kissed me and tugged at my T-shirt. Inside his bell-bottoms, his cock pulsed like the aurora borealis.

I pushed him away. "I'm not ready for that with you."

He rolled off with a sigh. He spooned me and ran gentle fingers through my hair. "I really dig you."

"I just broke up with my boyfriend."

"If you can't be with the one you love, love the one you're with."

"Not tonight."

I wasn't ready to fuck him, but I liked the way his body fit against mine. I liked the way it felt to be held. After a while, I placed one of his hands on my breast. He squeezed it and kissed the nape of my neck.

From inside the house, we heard Wendy cry out, "Yes, yes, fucking yes."

"Wow." I'd never experienced anything like that in the back of Bobby's Mustang.

"Sounds like she got hers," Jude said through a snicker.

His hardness pressed between my ass cheeks. He rolled my nipple in his fingers. I turned and sat up. He started to do the same, but I pinned him down with a hand on his chest. With my other hand, I unbuttoned his fly and reached inside.

"What are you doing?"

"You know what I'm doing."

"You don't have to, if . . ."

But I wanted to. "Just relax."

I wet my hand with saliva and began to stroke. His eyes rolled back in his head. His hips rose and fell to my rhythm.

"Fuck, yeah," he said.

I stroked harder, faster. "You like it?"

"Yeah, that's it. Don't stop."

Just before he shot, I pushed up my T-shirt and rubbed his flesh against mine.

"Jesus, yes, Jesus," he groaned as he gushed onto my breasts.

A low moan escaped my lips.

Then I was suddenly cold and wet in the night air. I kissed him, stood, and started across the yard.

"Hey," he called after me.

I wiped his stickiness on my cut-offs and kept walking. When I passed the porch of my new neighbors' house, Buck leaned against the railing. He was naked except for undershorts, and I tried not to look at his lean, hairy body. He waited until I was even with him before he spoke.

"Those nights in 'Nam," he said.

"What did you say?"

A faraway look haunted his face. "Those nights in 'Nam."

"What about them?"

"They were savage. The nights were fucking savage."

He looked like he was about to cry. Wendy strode through the door, wearing an Army shirt and nothing else. She took her man by the arm.

"C'mon, Buck. I'm here now."

He didn't resist when she steered him inside. She spoke to me over her shoulder. "He's still a little freaked about the war."

"Yeah, I guess."

"We'll see you tomorrow, right?"

I didn't have to think about it. "Definitely."

I sleepwalked through my days, serving burgers and fries. As soon as my shift ended, I was by Wendy's side. The men found work at one of the RV factories, so we had a little time to ourselves before they showed up hungry and horny.

"It doesn't have to be this way," Wendy explained, "working for The Establishment."

She was making brownies. But these weren't just any brownies. You'd walk on the moon after eating these brownies.

We'd met only nine days ago, but I felt like I'd known her forever. She was smarter than my mom, my teachers. She knew way more than my friends.

"So, how else would you get money?" I asked her.

"We don't need money. We can live off the land. Everyone contributes and we share. You do your thing. I do mine."

"I don't know how to do anything."

"Then you apprentice with someone like me who knows how to garden, who knows how to sew, who knows how to cook."

"I guess it could work."

"It has to. Otherwise, we'll blow ourselves up with The Bomb."

It wasn't a very pleasant alternative. "How long have you known Buck?"

"In this life, about a year."

"This life?"

"We knew each other in a previous life. It's why we're soul mates."

"He seems to make you happy."

She poured the brownie batter into a baking dish. We took turns licking the mixing bowl with a wooden spoon.

"He won a Silver Star in the war. He fucks like he fights."

"Wow," I managed. Nancy and Rhonda wouldn't even admit to having sex, much less talk about it like this.

"Are you fucking Jude, yet?" she asked.

I turned away. Jude and I were still stuck on hand jobs, but I didn't tell Wendy. "Not exactly."

She popped the brownies into the oven. "Have you ever had an orgasm?"

"A what? I don't know. I guess. Sure. Why not?"

She pulled herself onto the kitchen counter. "If you'd had one, you'd know. Have you ever rubbed yourself?"

"You mean . . ."

She hiked up her skirt, revealing a tangled thicket. She opened her legs, then used her fingers to spread her lips.

"Here's the spot," she said, touching the little bump at the top of her slit. "Rub yourself until you can't stand it. You'll know when to stop."

A red burn scorched my face. "I know that."

She gave me a sisterly smile and lowered her skirt. Her scent filled the room, making me blush even more. "We're all children of The Universe, sweetie. Go with it."

"Children of the universe?"

"Dust in the wind."

The next evening, Jude and I were on our blanket when we heard Wendy's cries.

We exchanged a knowing glance. "Let's go," I said.

I pulled him after me. We hunkered outside a bedroom window, peeking through the screen. We saw them in the candlelight, Wendy on all fours with Buck behind. Her pendulous breasts swung free as he plowed into her.

Jude's breath was hot in my ear. "Damn," he said.

I reached behind and lifted my skirt. Jude pushed my panties aside. He sought an entry I could no longer deny. His fingers in my pussy sang a squishy tune.

Buck smacked Wendy's ass hard enough to make her yelp.

I fumbled with Jude's belt. His cock sprang free.

"I want you," he whispered.

I wasn't thinking about Bobby anymore. I really wasn't thinking about Jude either, but I wanted his cock.

"Do it," I said. "Go ahead, do it."

He pushed and I pushed back. He fucked me standing up, slow and sweet. On the other side of the screen, Buck's tight butt worked—*slap, slap, slap*. Wendy ground against him. Suddenly, her belly clenched. She writhed and grunted like a construction worker.

I wanted some of that.

I slid a hand inside my panties. While Jude pumped, I rubbed.

Wendy flipped onto her back and Buck knelt beside her. She took him in her mouth. He pumped in and out, then threw back his head and squirted white and hot across her lips. She gathered his cream in her hands and licked her fingers clean.

Behind me, Jude shuddered and gasped. I felt that quickening between my thighs, but this time, I didn't let go. I rubbed and rubbed, overcome with longing. It began like the rumble of distant artillery fire. Red and green tracers zipped past and shells burst in a dazzle. The night exploded into a thousand heartless shards. My knees buckled and Jude held on to keep me from falling.

Yes, yes, fucking yes.

They'd intended to stay the summer and earn a little money before moving on, but The Man was on to Jude. Blue suits showed up in town asking about hippies.

"We're outta here tonight," Wendy told me.

The guys had already taken the minibus to the lot by the creek for a paint-job makeover.

"I've got some things to do," I told her. "Don't you dare leave before I get back."

I called in sick and rode my bike to town. I hated that job anyway. My first stop was the bank. I'd saved most of my wages and tips—$500. I kept $450 for myself and used the balance to replace Bobby's class ring. Sort of. The man at the pawnshop didn't have this year's ring, but he had plenty from a few years earlier.

It would have to do.

Then I went home and packed.

Then I wrote Bobby a letter.

I wrote that if we'd really been meant for each other, he'd have found a way to stay home instead of going off to war, he'd have spent his last three weeks before Basic with me instead of Mike, and he'd have given the Mustang to me instead of selling it to the first guy who answered his ad. If we'd really been meant for each other, we'd probably have met in a previous life.

Finally, I wrote that he should be careful in The Nam.

I'd heard the nights were savage there, fucking savage.

I left my mom a note too. I was going to San Francisco, but she didn't have to worry, because there were gentle people there, people who wanted only peace and love. We were all children of the universe.

I left Dunlap that evening in the minibus, repainted a dull black to hide the psychedelic hippie shit underneath.

Wendy lit a reefer and passed it around. Buck pointed the minibus into the sunset. Jude held my hand, looking more stoned than usual.

Dunlap disappeared behind us.

And the rest is history.

A LOVER IN THE HOUSE OF SPIES

My mother was a spy. Or maybe just a bored professional with an overactive imagination.

All my sister and I could say for sure was that she traveled often, claimed she was with the State Department, and kept a journal. She and our father led separate lives until he died a few years before she passed. He had his golf, his business associates, and his other women. She had her work, her books, and her daughters.

But never other men, so far as we knew.

We found the journal in a trunk along with her wedding dress, personal correspondence to grandmothers and aunts, and old photos. Jen, two years older than me, the proper banker with glasses and perfect nails, refused to read it.

"She was a private woman, Kate. She would never have wanted this."

But if our mother hadn't wanted us to read her journal, why hadn't she destroyed it? Why had she left the key to the trunk in a lockbox with instructions to her lawyer to turn the key over to us?

"Besides," Jen pointed out, "she was demented in her final years. Demented, Kate."

But the dates on the journal weren't from our mother's declining years. She'd been a healthy, vibrant forty-something between 1970 and 1972.

"You should be ashamed of yourself, Kate. Let's put it back."

"Sure, whatever you say."

But I scooped up the journal when she wasn't looking. I took it home to my apartment near the university. I read it by a dim light, in bed, with the covers pulled tight.

June 20, 1970
Flight over the Atlantic, Lisbon to DC

Our Chief of Station here is a lecherous buggerer who prefers underage boys to women. The KGB is at the other end of the spectrum. Their man, Boris Poderezky, touched my ass on the way to dinner. Throughout a meal of vodka, squid, and sausages, he stared at my breasts as if they were the first he'd ever seen. By the end of the evening, we struck a deal. I'm to run a "honey trap" on Kamenev, the Soviet scientist suspected of selling nuclear secrets to the Libyans. Once he confesses and exposes his connections, Boris will close the trap. I have a girl in mind, a Yalie who recently joined the Clandestine Service. Kamenev will never be able to resist her.

Streeter worked at the Student Union as a janitor. He was years younger than me with unruly black hair, wild eyes, and a hard, tattooed body. I picked him up over Christmas break, when not many students were around. I flashed him my panties while grading papers in the lounge. He asked if he could buy me coffee. Then he asked if I had a lover. When I said no, he placed a hand on my knee under the table.

A rough, calloused hand.

We kept our trysts secret, using empty rooms in the hotel wing to which he had keys. What would the dean say if he knew a full professor was sleeping with a janitor no older than her students? Besides, Streeter had a girlfriend.

June 27, 1970
Palácio Belmonte—Lisbon, Portugal

The Director himself intervened and said no "honey traps" using untested Yalies. We're still running the honey trap, but now I'm the honey. It's not like I haven't done this before. Good thing Kamenev is older, fifty if he's a day, because I turn forty next month. I'm not that sweet, young Yalie, but I still have a good figure. I just left Kamenev at the bar downstairs. Boris tracked him here where he's speaking at a conference. The Mossad (Israeli Intelligence) has also reported attendance by a Libyan named Muhammed al Mujaahid. We believe al Mujaahid may be Kamenev's contact. What kind of man sells nuclear secrets to terrorists? An intelligent man, a handsome man, a quiet-spoken man. A man who knows how to treat a lady. (If this wasn't just a job, I could probably get to like this Kamenev). Anyway, the hook is set. He asked me to join him for dinner tomorrow night. He thinks I'm a rich American widow on holiday.

Streeter and I lay naked in bed. I'd just ridden him hard, bouncing on his long, slick cock until we both came. He was smoking in a non-smoking room. He told me I was the best pussy he'd ever had. When I asked why, he said it was because

I needed it so much, because I'd do anything he said. Also, because of my glasses. He didn't expect a smart girl to like it so much.

He mashed out his cigarette and pushed a finger that smelled like tobacco between my lips. He moved it in and out while staring into my eyes behind my glasses. I flicked his finger with my tongue, sucked it like a cock. He watched, fascinated, his jaw slack. He sat up in bed, hard again, and knelt beside me.

"Do yourself while I fuck your mouth," he said.

I opened my legs, dipped inside my slit, and smeared pussy nectar on my clit. I gave my mouth to him. With my free hand, I held his balls.

He pumped in and out. I rubbed furiously. I made myself a vessel. I gagged when he came. He withdrew and sprayed my face and glasses.

"Oh, yeah, baby," I managed.

I rubbed and rubbed and rubbed. I screamed when I came. I didn't give a shit who heard.

June 27, 1970
Dom Pedro Palace—Lisbon, Portugal

Dinner was exquisite. The two bottles of red wine, luscious as the countryside. Afterwards, we talked and drank some more, enjoying the view from the highest hill in Lisbon. We overlooked the city and the ocean beyond. You could fall in love here with the right person. Kamenev is erudite and soft-spoken. He's married, of course, but like many marriages, his has lost steam over the years. He told me that he's a scientist, but withheld that he is the depository of secrets that could destroy the world. We're making slow progress, but I have only two more nights with him. He walked me to my room and kissed me at my door. I pushed my breasts against him.

My psychotherapist was a thin, bird-like woman. She wore her hair in a tight bun. Reading glasses perched on a long, narrow nose. Her dark eyes burned bright. "And this man, do you feel affection for him?"

I considered the question. I didn't dislike Streeter, but neither did I find him an interesting companion. He was not all that imaginative in bed and hadn't read a book since high school. He was barely alert to current events, more informed about the drinking habits of his coarse friends than the War on Terror or presidential politics.

"I like fucking him," I said.

"What about his girlfriend?"

"What about her?"

"Do you ever consider that he's betraying her? That this is the kind of man you've chosen to engage with?"

"We're not engaging. We're fucking. Besides, what goes on between him and his girlfriend is none of my business."

She scribbled in her notebook. "Your last two relationships have been with men well below your social status. There was that traveling salesman, that graduate student. Why do you think you're drawn to men like this?"

I shrugged. I was the one paying her $150 an hour. "I don't know. Their expectations are low. It's easy."

She eyed me over her readers. "It's risky, promiscuous, and demeaning."

"Maybe I like playing the slut."

"And why is that?"

I'd been in therapy before. She wanted me to say it was because I was insecure and had low self-esteem. She wanted me to say it was because my parents had been self-involved narcissists.

I was not going to make it that easy for her. "Because I like it dirty. It's more exciting that way."

She didn't blink. "But why is that?"

I leaned forward. "Because my mother was a spy and lied about everything."

She set her notebook aside and checked her clock. "We'll have to explore that next time."

June 28, 1970
Dom Pedro Palace—Lisbon, Portugal

I couldn't sleep last night, thinking of the job ahead. I will seduce Kamenev. I will ensnare him with my sex. Then, I will tease out his secrets. I've done it before. I will do it again. It's a job. But if it's just a job, why am I humping the bed? Why am I wet with desire? What kind of lover is he? Kind and caring? Rough and demanding? What unrequited desires haunt his soul? Will he want my mouth, my cunt, my tits, my ass? As morning draws near, I position a pillow on the bed in front of the mirror. As the sepia tones of dawn bathe the room, I ride the pillow as if it were Kamenev. Fuck me, I groan to my reflection. Come on, fuck me.

My sister called about the journal. She'd returned to the house and visited the attic in search of old photos. She noticed the journal missing.

"What journal?"

"You know damn well what journal."

"Look . . ."

"Always with the lies, Kate. Always with the secrets."

"Well, if you knew, why'd you ask?"

June 29, 1970
Dom Pedro Palace—Lisbon, Portugal

What now, my poor, sweet Kamenev? Last night, dinner, wine, and dancing. Then to my room. Once inside, I dropped to my knees, unzipped and unfurled him. I slid my dress off my shoulders. He sat on the bed, me at his feet.

"Your breasts," he whispered.

He kneaded and tweaked, while I licked and bobbed. He thrust into the cleavage, hard and slippery with my saliva.

"Yes," he said behind closed eyes.

I should have known—a tit man.

I gathered him into me, rising and falling. He grunted and spurted, then leaned forward and kissed me on the lips. He lifted me up, laid me across the bed, and pushed my skirts over my hips. Then he devoured me, flicking mercilessly at that most sensitive flesh, probing me with his fingers. Until, until. My God, so shattering.

Forty years old and I've missed so much in my own tepid marriage. Afterwards, as we lay smoking Turkish cigarettes, he confessed. The Libyan was blackmailing him. His daughter at the Sorbonne was in danger if he didn't help the terrorists.

Streeter had another woman. I'd seen them together on campus. She was pretty and blonde. She laughed when he talked to her. I never laughed at his stupid jokes.

This new man, I met at the Holiday Inn. He was a retired businessman, cool and self-possessed.

"I know you," he said over our second drink.

"Really? Have we met before?"

"No, but I know you. You've been looking for a man who will use you properly. All those others were amateurs."

"Use me?"

The back of his hand traced my jawline. "Like the slut you are."

I felt loose and uncertain inside. "You don't . . ."

"You want to be used, don't you?"

"Well . . ."

"I'll take you lower than you've ever imagined. I'll punish you if you don't comply."

"I . . ."

"You've been waiting for this all your life."

I glanced about the bar. "Will I be safe?"

"Only as safe as you want to be."

My heart thundered in my chest. "But you said punish."

"That's what happens to bad girls, isn't it?"

I bit my lower lip. "God yes."

July 5, 1970
A Safe House—Tel Aviv, Israel

The Israelis. They shot the Libyan and abducted Kamenev and his daughter. I'm taking him back to the States. Boris is furious at the double cross. Late at night, Kamenev visits my bed. He rests his head on my bosom. I hold his cock in my hand, a bird about to take wing.

My mother's affair lasted two years, at least. After two years, the journal ended. I stopped seeing my therapist. My Master suggested I don't need her anymore.

Snowbound

Kate folded jeans and cords and placed them in her old Land's End bag. She added turtlenecks, sweaters, and socks. Although they were leaving for "up north" within the hour, Josh's clothes still lay in a pile. Since she'd stopped picking up after him, he'd resorted to what he called recycling.

It wasn't all that charming.

But she'd be damned if she'd help him out. And she'd be damned if they left a minute after three o'clock. If he wasn't packed and ready to go, he'd have to spend the weekend in the clothes on his back.

Finished with her own packing, she went to the window and looked out onto the red-brick street. Most of the students had departed for home and the upcoming holiday earlier in the week. The usually bustling campus was deserted, except for faculty and a few graduate students like her and Josh. The emptiness of the campus was accentuated by the bare trees and cold, gray skies. Fallen brown leaves gathered in gutters, swept up by a cruel wind.

Snow threatened.

That's why they needed to leave on time. Otherwise, they risked being stranded in the snowstorm that brewed to the north and west. And, God knew, they couldn't afford a night on the road. Besides, about the last thing she wanted was to spend a night alone in a hotel room with Josh. Here, in this sad, little house on 8th Street, she could avoid lying down next to her husband by pretending to fall asleep at her computer. She could storm into the living room or lock him out of the bedroom.

But stuck in a hotel room, there would be no avoiding him and no avoiding the chasm that had opened between them.

A chasm of his making.

She saw him coming, gangly arms swinging, head bare, his backpack weighing him down. Although four years had passed since their marriage, he didn't look a day older. Unlike Kate, who was struggling to complete her doctoral thesis, Josh thrived in academia. Even with the constant three-day beard and long, black hair that hadn't been cut in months, he looked as smart and handsome as the day they'd met.

But it wasn't his looks that had attracted her to him. It was his keen mind. From the moment they'd met, she'd wanted to bend her body to that intellect, rub her sex against it like a cat rubbing against a warm pant-leg.

She might know French existentialist literature, but he knew quantum physics and understood the way subatomic particles fit together to create the universe.

It was like being married to God.

He pushed through the door, accompanied by a gust of cold air. "Hey," he said.

She frowned at him. "You've got five minutes to get your shit together."

The other woman—barely more than a girl, actually—had been an undergraduate student in the physics lab Josh taught. Sasha was Asian with long, black hair, almond-shaped eyes, and unexpectedly large breasts for someone so petite. Kate discovered their affair through a video clip attached to an e-mail sent by Sasha's distraught boyfriend.

Han secretly taped them making love with a well-placed nanny cam.

The video showed Josh and Sasha entering an off-campus apartment. Dressed in a short skirt and blouse, Sasha led him by the hand, giggling. She turned and they kissed. His hands slid down her back and over her buttocks. She unbuttoned his shirt and kissed his chest. She sat on the bed and unzipped his jeans. She took his cock in her mouth and began sucking—all the while, those beautiful eyes searched his face.

Josh told her to get on her hands and knees. She obeyed, burying her face in a pillow, thrusting her buttocks high in the air. He lifted her skirt, revealing that she wore no panties. He swatted her hard enough to leave a visible handprint. She yelped into the pillow.

"You've been a naughty girl, haven't you?"

She turned her face to reply. "I didn't get my homework in on time."

He smacked her again. "You'll do better next time, won't you?"

"Yes, yes."

He dipped his hand into the furrow between her legs. "You're wet, little girl."

"You make me wet, professor."

He smacked her harder than before. "You're such a nasty little girl."

"Oh, yes I am."

Josh pumped in and out. She pushed against his fingers. "Is this why you didn't get your homework done? You were too busy playing?"

"I masturbate and think of you all the time, professor."

Josh applied his free hand to her thighs and ass. Red marks appeared. Sasha wailed.

"You fuck yourself in class, while watching me, don't you?"

"I get so wet, listening to your lectures. I squeeze my legs together until I come."

"You do it in the bathroom after class, don't you?"

"I can't wait to get to the bathroom and shove my brush inside my cunt. I wish it was your cock."

"You play with yourself in the library when you should be studying, don't you?"

"I play under my skirt until my cubicle smells like sex."

Josh worked his fingers faster. Sasha's movements became frenzied. Her face darkened.

"You think of me when your boyfriend fucks you, don't you?"

"He doesn't fuck me like you do."

"Are you ready to be fucked hard and true, little girl?"

"Yes, yes, yes. Fuck me, professor. Teach me how it's done."

Still in his jeans, Josh knelt behind her, slipped on a condom, and pushed inside. She wailed louder and shuddered against him.

Josh smacked both cheeks. He made a ponytail of her hair and pulled back on it. "You were supposed to wait until I said you could come, you little slut."

"Please, professor. I couldn't help myself."

Josh drove his cock deep and hard. Sasha whimpered and spasmed again.

Josh rocked against her. "You want my cum, nasty girl?"

"Oh, God yes. Drown me in it, professor."

He withdrew and removed the condom. "You're so nasty," he said, stroking himself.

"Do it, professor. Please, come on my ass."

"Finger yourself, little girl. Show me how bad you want it."

Sasha rubbed between her legs. She pinched a nipple through her blouse. The squishy sounds of her arousal filled the air. Behind her, Josh jerked and bucked. His face contorted and semen leapt from his cock. It sprayed across her ass and onto her lower back. She cried out and orgasmed a third time.

After they'd both regained their senses, Josh chuckled softly. He lay down beside her and kissed her mouth.

"You are so hot," he said.

"I love that game," she said with a giggle.

"We should do this in the classroom," Josh said. He stuffed his cock inside his jeans.

"Oh, I'd like that," Sasha said, rising onto one elbow.

"I better get going," Josh said. "I'm picking Kate up from the library."

"You better save yourself for me, mister."

"Don't worry about that."

Here, the video clip ended.

Kate watched it, then watched it again. She confronted Josh when he returned home that evening. While she stood over him weeping softly, he hung his head.

"I'm sorry," he said. "I'm sorry, Kate."

"Fuck you," she told him.

The snow started on the north side of Indianapolis. By the time they turned off of I-465 onto Highway 31, the sky was dark with flurries. Kate called her mother in South Bend. She could imagine the woman, a high school teacher, sitting on a barstool in the kitchen of the house where Kate had grown up.

"Mom," Kate said. "This is looking pretty bad here. How is it by you?"

"It's coming down pretty hard. We've already got three inches and they say we could have a foot by morning. They say the temps are supposed to drop overnight."

"A foot," Kate said to Josh out of the corner of her mouth.

"We better find a place to stay."

"Josh thinks we should pull over," Kate told her mother.

"How's the road?"

"We can still see it."

"I hate for you to miss being here with the family tomorrow morning . . ."

"I hate to miss Grandma's holiday waffles. What does Dad think?"

"Here, talk to him."

Kate waited for the gruff voice. He was the owner of the local Toyota dealership. "If you don't make it tonight, you'll miss the holiday. There's another storm on the way after this one."

"There's another storm on the way," Kate relayed to Josh.

"You've got front-wheel drive in that Camry," her dad said. "Just remind Josh to turn into the skids."

"He's a physicist, Dad. He probably knows that."

"Anyway."

"I'll call when we get closer." She closed her cell phone.

"We should stop," Josh said. "It's getting hard to see. The wind is picking up."

Kate stared into the swirling chaos of white beyond the windshield. "I want to make it home for the holiday."

"So, what's next?" she'd asked two days after showing him the video clip. "If you want to be with her, I understand."

"I don't want to be with anyone but you."

"That's why you were fucking Sasha, right?"

"It wasn't like that. I didn't go looking for it."

Kate stood in the doorway, her arms crossed over her breasts. She'd hardly slept or ate. When she wasn't crying, she was pacing the floor, trying to find the courage to leave.

"You didn't go looking for it?"

"I'm not saying I'm innocent. I made a mistake. But it was a one-time thing. It won't happen again."

"Professor," she said, mocking Sasha's words. He wasn't really a professor. He was waiting to hear back from the universities to which he'd applied for a position.

"Kate, please."

"I don't know if I can trust you."

He looked awful. She supposed he hadn't slept either. "You know I'm not that kind of guy."

At least that was true. Both of them were smart and physically attractive enough, but also socially awkward. They'd studied together and been friends for months before going on a real date. He'd taken her to a tele-lecture by Stephen Hawking. A week later, she'd invited him to a reading by and reception for Joyce Carol Oates.

While the famous author read from her latest novel, he'd taken her hand. Later, in his dorm room, after he'd finished describing string theory to her, she'd stood and silently stripped. She'd decided it was time to lose her virginity and this was the young man she wanted to lose it to. Ten minutes later, with him spent in the condom she'd supplied, he confessed it was his first time too.

His fling with Sasha was as much a betrayal of their shared geekiness as it was their marriage.

"I don't know who you are anymore."

Josh sighed. "Do you want me to leave?"

"Not yet. I'm not done punishing you."

North of Peru and Grissom Air Force Base, the wind picked up. It buffeted the secondhand Camry, making it difficult for Josh to keep the tires in the ruts.

"Shit," Josh said. "I can't see anything."

The temperature had dropped fifteen degrees in the last hour. It hovered just above ten degrees. The wind was blowing harder, making it impossible to see. They lost the taillights of the semi-truck they'd been following for the last hour.

"This isn't good," Kate said.

"What's the next town? Maybe we can find a room there."

"There's nothing for forty miles."

"Goddamnit."

Out of the white, the lights of the semi suddenly appeared again—right in front of them. Josh swerved to prevent a collision.

"Watch out, watch out," Kate cried.

The brakes locked and the car went into a skid. It slid onto the shoulder and into a ditch. Josh gunned the motor and tried to climb out, but it was no use. The Camry fishtailed before coming to rest against a fencepost in a snowbank eight feet below the grade of the road.

"Holy shit," he said.

Kate drew a deep breath. At least the car was still running. "We'll need a tow truck to get out of here."

"We won't get one tonight."

"I didn't say tonight." It came out harsher than she'd intended. "I didn't mean tonight."

Kate opened her cell phone, searched for a signal, and found none. "I can't even call anyone."

Josh stared straight ahead, thinking it through. His mind worked like a computer. He'd calculate their options, analyze the risk and reward, and come up with a solution.

"You stay here," he said. "I'll go up to the road and get help. We'll catch a ride and figure it out from there."

The wind rocked the car like a toy. She guessed the windchill to be well below zero. The cold leaked through the cracks and crevices.

"You can't stay out there long."

"We can't stay here. We only have a half-tank of gas."

Josh searched his pockets for gloves. He pulled his sock cap over his ears. "I'll be back."

"Be careful."

For a moment, she thought he might kiss her. She was relieved when he opened the door and stepped outside. The blast of cold air took her breath away.

In the two months following Josh's fling, they'd twice visited a thin-lipped marriage counselor who wanted to know if either of them had been abused as children. They'd tried talking it out like intelligent adults, but he'd turned inward, reduced to grunts and shrugs. She'd become sarcastic. Is that what he really wanted—an eighteen-year-old who played the slutty schoolgirl? The kinkiest thing he'd ever wanted from her had been a blow job on the kitchen table or a slick, soapy fuck against the shower wall.

As the weeks passed, they'd been reduced to going through the motions, avoiding each other in the bathroom, sleeping in separate rooms, eating alone on the run.

Only in the last few days had she realized she was putting off a decision about them until after the holidays. She wanted one more holiday dinner with him, one more morning around the tree, one more evening in front of the fire. She hoped to give the holiday a chance to bridge the chasm that yawned between them.

Now it looked like she'd lost that chance. Instead of the healing warmth of family, fire, and good food, they were facing cold and snow.

Sitting alone in the car, pummeled by the wind, unable to see three feet in front of her, the knowledge settled in. It was here in this snowdrift that her marriage would end.

Ten minutes later, he was back, snow-covered and red-faced. "Sonofabitch," he said. "It's cold."

"Any luck?"

Josh reclined against the headrest and removed his stocking cap. "Nothing's moving. I think they've closed the road."

"So, we're stuck here?"

"Looks that way."

"For the night?"

"At least."

"So, what do you suggest?"

"I suggested pulling over an hour ago."

She frowned. "That doesn't help."

"It's nine o'clock and we've only got about four hours of gas. We have to make it last. We'll run the car for a while, then leave it off for as long as we can stand. Hopefully, we'll find a way out of here come daylight."

"Not much of a plan."

"It's the best I can do. You got anything better?"

They sat there for a long moment in their separate seats before Kate spoke again, "We could cover the windows with our clothes to keep the wind out. There's a blanket in the backseat. We could cover up and use our body heat."

"I didn't want to suggest it," Josh said. "I thought you'd think I was taking advantage of the situation."

Kate pulled her sweatshirt over her head, cracked the window, stuffed the sweatshirt into the crack, then closed the window tight again.

"Look," she said, "we're talking survival."

Josh peeled off his old parka and jammed it against the windshield. "We're losing a lot of heat there."

Kate wriggled out of her jeans and flannel shirt and used them to insulate the other side of the windshield. Josh plugged up the rear windows with his sweatshirt and chinos. When they were down to their undies and the inside of the car was as hot as an oven, Josh switched off the car and they crawled into the backseat.

He lay down first, his knees bent double to accommodate his height. Kate lay on top, pulling the blanket after her. Her head came to rest on his chest where it always did when they snuggled.

Despite their efforts at insulating the windows, Kate's nose and feet were cold right away. "It feels like outer space out there."

"We're caught in a deep low pressure. It invites the arctic cold and arctic cold is about as close to outer space as it gets on Earth."

"My mom will worry when I don't call."

"It can't be helped. Maybe you can get a signal after the storm blows through."

"You think this will blow through?"

"It's an Alberta clipper. In a few more hours, the wind will die, the sky will clear, and the real cold will settle in."

"The real cold?"

"Probably drop below zero."

Kate snuggled closer.

She must have fallen asleep. She was awakened by Josh. The car was warm again, but he was turning it off. He settled next to her. Through the rear window, she could see stars. The wind's howl had ceased.

"What time is it?" she asked.

"About one o'clock. It's down to ten below."

"I should try my mom."

"There's still no signal."

"How much gas is left?"

"A good quarter tank."

"It's so clear," she said. "There are so many stars."

Josh pointed. "There are the Big and Little Dippers. There is Gemini. And Orion's Belt is over there."

"What's that? It looks like something spilled."

"That's the Milky Way. I used to camp in the woods at night, so I could study the stars and constellations. You get a good look at it from the Rockies."

He'd grown up in Colorado, the child of hippies. She could imagine him, the little boy Josh, sitting in the deep darkness under a blanket of stars. She could imagine the mop of hair, the brown eyes filled with wonder. She pressed her nose into the nape of his neck.

"It's like ice," he said.

She pressed her feet against his. "My feet too."

He pulled away. "You're always cold."

"Good thing you're always warm."

"Yeah, I guess."

"So, you think we're going to make it."

"The gas should last until morning. The plows should be out then."

"But we'll miss the holiday."

"We could still make it for the holiday," he said, "if we got an early tow and hit the road before that next storm."

"Those are some big *ifs*. Besides, it's not that big of a deal to you, is it?"

"I wanted one more holiday with you. I wanted a fire with your family. I wanted to sing around the piano. I wanted one more drink with your dad."

She propped herself up on one elbow. "What do you mean, one more?"

"That's what you've decided, isn't it?"

"I never said that."

"You didn't have to."

"I haven't made a decision. I was waiting until afterwards."

A long moment passed in the dark. "I wish I could go back," Josh said. "I wish I could erase the last few months."

"Not possible."

"It was stupid, Kate. I made a mistake."

"Obviously, I wasn't enough for you."

"That's not true. You were so caught up in your thesis I didn't think you wanted me."

"You're saying it's my fault? You're saying I wasn't available to you? You're saying I wasn't giving you enough sex? That's bullshit. I'd have done anything you asked."

"I'm not saying it's your fault. But why should I always have to ask?"

"You're the one who wasn't getting all you wanted."

"Look, I'm just saying I felt like you'd already left me for your books."

Kate frowned. "It's not as easy for me as it is for you. Anyway, you should've said something."

"I did, Kate. All summer long I tried to get you to go away with me. I tried to get you to take a break."

She sat up and wrapped her arms about her. The sultry heat of the summer seemed ages ago. Looking back on it, all she remembered was the library, a cubicle, and Sartre's "Being and Nothingness."

"So that makes it all right for you to fuck around?"

"I'm not saying it makes it all right. I'm saying I felt like you'd left me for those French beatniks—Sartre and Camus. I'm saying I was vulnerable when Sasha came on to me."

She looked away. "Here's the thing—I don't know if I can get past it."

Josh reached out and caressed her cheek with the back of his hand. "I know I've hurt you, Kate. I'd do anything to undo that, but it's up to you to give us another chance."

His voice cracked in a way she'd never heard. When she turned back to him, a tear illuminated in the star-shine coursed down his cheek. She felt an unexpected stab of sympathy and, for the first time, realized that he'd been wounded by all of this too. She reached out and flicked his tear away. Then she bent to him and kissed where it had been, salty and cool.

"I want to give us another chance. I just don't know how."

Josh pushed his hair off his forehead. "Remember that first holiday at your folks' house, before we were even engaged. They put me in the basement and you slept in your old bedroom."

"I waited until I heard my dad snoring, then I sneaked downstairs."

"I couldn't sleep."

"We were so afraid of being caught."

"You thought we'd be too noisy if we actually did it."

"We worked things out." She remembered. It was the first time they'd masturbated together. He'd watched her, awestruck, then he'd done himself while she spooned him and whispered his name.

He reached out and held her face in his hands. "I've missed you, Kate. I've missed us."

She stroked his cheek, brought her lips to his, and kissed softly. "I've missed you too."

He slipped out of his undershirt and unhooked her bra. Her breath was visible, her nipples stiff with cold and anticipation. She pressed her breasts against his warm chest. Then, for the first time in months, she kissed him deeply, their tongues swirling. He returned the kiss, his mouth hungry on hers, his hands greedy for her body.

"It's been so long," he said.

She felt it too. Blood pounded in her ears. She pressed her pelvis against his thigh, her panties damp with need. She reached below his flat belly, grasping for him through his boxer shorts. He was thick and hard.

"Don't talk," she said.

He cupped her breasts, squeezed, and lifted. He flicked at her nipples with his tongue. He sucked like a babe long denied.

Dizzy with lust, she worked his cock free. She turned and lowered her face to him. She took him in her mouth and groaned at how good it felt to have him there again. She sucked and tasted his salty essence.

His hands pushed her panties aside. Three fingers opened her and found her wetness. He teased her most sensitive flesh.

She cried out, pushed his boxers to his knees, and nuzzled his furry testicles with her lips and tongue. She stroked him while rocking against his insistent fingers.

He brought his lips and tongue to her pussy. He licked and sucked like a thirsty man in the desert. His tongue assaulted her clit, circling and flicking until she squirmed and filled that cold, moonless night with her moans. The tension mounted and she gave herself to him, wet and sloppy and shameless, her orgasm beginning deep inside, then emanating outward, wave after wave. Her belly clenched; her thighs shuddered. She pushed into his face, grinding out her pleasure, and it was *oh god, oh god, oh god*—over and over and over.

While she found her breath again, he continued to lick and suckle her pussy sweetly. His fingertips made circles on her buttocks. She took him deep in her mouth. She tightened her lips around him and sucked hard as she withdrew—quarter inch by sweet quarter inch. She tightened her grip on his balls, holding them in the palm of her hand like a quivering baby bird.

She flicked under the head while jacking him, slowly at first, then faster. She took him deep again, shameless still in her lust, until she felt his cock thicken with cum, until she heard the telltale *yes, baby, yes*! Only then did she hold the head between her lips like a fat straw, stroking him, drinking him, squirt after squirt, tasting him warm and salty and slightly bitter. And she kept at it, even after he'd given her all he had to give, until the next time—even after he'd gone soft in her mouth, even after he reached for her and said he just wanted to hold her.

She kept at it, because he was her man and she was his woman and they'd found each other again in a snowbank as cold as the universe.

He awoke the next morning before she did. Frost had formed on the whiskers under his nose. Naked, he leaned into the front seat and restarted the car. She felt stiff and achy. They'd made love twice more during the night and the muscles in her thighs and buttocks were stretched and sore. Once, she rode him, bouncing and calling his name while he clawed her backside. Another time, he took her from behind, her cheek pressed against the ice forming inside the car's window.

She reached between his legs and touched him. He slapped her hand away playfully. A pink sunrise revealed the fencepost they'd nearly crashed into. Beyond the fence, drifts of snow, sculpted by the wind, stretched as far as she could see.

"We should get dressed," Josh told her.

"Listen," Kate said.

Above and in the distance was the sound of a truck grinding through its gears.

"Come on," Josh said. "They're plowing the road."

A few minutes later, they were dressed and he was pulling her up the incline. The road was unrecognizable, but from the south, the lights of two massive snowplows, working side by side, sped toward them. The plows sprayed snow onto the shoulders on each side of the northbound lanes.

Josh waved and brought both plows to a halt. A man in orange coveralls and a parka climbed out of the cab closest to them. While Josh spoke with the man, Kate tried her cell again. Up on the road, she found the signal she'd been denied in the ditch.

"Kate, oh my God," her mother said.

She explained the situation.

"We've got lots of snow," her mother said, "but the roads are clear."

"They don't expect the next storm until tomorrow," she heard her father say. "Tell Josh they've got a window."

"We'll hold off until tonight, when you get here," her mother said.

Josh waved her over. "Hold on," Kate told her mom.

"There's a tow truck on the way," Josh said. "The guy says they'll have the northbound roads cleared from here to South Bend by the time we're out. We could be at your folks by noon."

The sun's brightness on the new-fallen snow was blinding. Steam rose from the newly cleared pavement.

"What do you want to do?" she asked.

He jammed his hands into his pocket. "I just want to be with you."

Kate weighed the alternatives. "Mom, we're going back to Bloomington. We don't want to get caught in that next storm. We've had about all the snow we can handle for one holiday."

Her words were met with a long pause before her mother spoke, "Well, we understand. We'll miss you, but we understand."

"We'll definitely be home for spring break."

"We'll be here."

They said good-bye and Kate closed the phone. She snaked an arm around Josh's waist. He pulled her close.

"Are you okay with this?" he asked. "I know how much the holidays mean to you."

"Our holiday was last night."

Josh leaned over and kissed her forehead. "Does that mean you're willing to give us a second chance?"

"If you are."

"What do you mean?"

"The next time Sartre gets too big in our lives, tell me straight. Push me against a wall and make me understand."

"All right."

"The next time you're feeling vulnerable, sweep me up and throw me on the bed. Fuck the living shit out of me."

"All right."

"And if you want to spank someone, spank me, professor. Spank me hard."

Josh blushed and pawed the ice. "All right."

The snowplows roared back to life. Josh led her out of their path. As they swept by, the driver closest to them hollered out, "Happy holidays."

Kate waved. "Happy holidays to you."

VOYEUR NATION

You reach a certain age and start looking over your shoulder. I was turning thirty-six, so maybe I was there. I was trying to be more responsible, more goal-oriented, more focused. My New Year's resolutions reflected it—eat healthier food, exercise more, save for a rainy day, find a boyfriend.

Not that I had exactly squandered my life—I'd made it through both law school and culinary school. I'd published several stories and a novel, and I'd had at least two meaningful (well, sort of) relationships.

Still, here I was, living on Manhattan Beach, house-sitting for my brother and his wife, and working on a second novel I couldn't finish. Here I was, living off the sale of ad copy and marketing collateral to multi-national corporations that exploited their employees and overpaid their executives. Here I was, chaste as a nun, having been without a lover for four months, three days, and sixteen hours.

But who was counting?

Recognizing that I was in serious jeopardy of losing it, I bought a Blackberry on which I set up a daily schedule. I opened and installed my two-year-old copy of Quicken. I set up a budget and online bill-pay. I gave up fun-sized Snickers and Fat Boy ice cream sandwiches. I pasted sticky notes of encouragement on the fridge and e-mailed myself "To Do" lists. I began saying hello to strangers on The Strand and joined a Writers' Workshop at Barnes and Noble.

I attacked each day with purpose. I was on a mission to get my shit together.

Until the kids next door arrived. Not that they were really kids. So far as I could tell, Susan and Ian were in their mid-twenties. But they seemed like kids with all that youthful exuberance, fresh-faced curiosity, and energetic sex.

They moved in at the beginning of last month. Prior to their arrival, the place was occupied by its previous owner—a lecherous, aging Baby Boomer by the name of Old Dan—who kept a close eye on my comings and goings, always lurking about, and always knocking on the door just as I was stepping out of the shower. He seemed to know my newfound routine better than I did.

He'd call out, "You're starting your run kinda late, aren't you?" Or, "Don't you usually write on the deck on Tuesdays?"

Creepy, huh?

Actually, I kept an eye on him too. Him and his bright-green Speedo that failed to hide the swagger of his dick and balls, and the yawning crack of his ass when he leaned over to water his begonia. Him and that wretched witch who visited for fuck-buddy sex every Tuesday and Thursday. Him and that little hottie down the street who was forever whirlpooling in the altogether, jilling off in the jets of Old Dan's Jacuzzi for half the world to see. And, oh yeah, him and the slut from the coffee shop—the one who must not have known there were other ways to access a man other than on one's knees.

Not that I was looking or anything.

Anyway, Old Dan and his Speedo moved out and Susan and Ian moved in.

Privacy was a challenge in our neighborhood. The homes were built in close proximity. People often left their windows and doors open, due to the year-round warm weather. Neighbors' roofs overlooked patios and bathrooms, and allowed for peeking into bedrooms and kitchens.

You never knew what you were going to see.

Or reveal.

I first became aware of Susan and Ian's activities shortly after they moved in. I came home around dinnertime, ordered pizza, and enjoyed it with a bottle of wine. After watching the sun set into the Pacific from my patio, I checked my container garden. It was while weeding a rose that I heard sounds coming from my neighbors' roof.

You know the kind of sounds I mean.

A sharp, quick exhalation followed by an "oh baby." I slithered into the shadows and positioned myself for a look. There was Susan, brown eyes closed, blonde hair cascading onto her shoulders, mouth open in an "O," and bare breasts swaying.

She grasped the railing and humped hard. I couldn't see below her waist or into the darkness behind, but I imagined Ian there, somehow involved.

Based on the rising crescendo of Susan's cries, whatever he was doing was working. After she came with a high-pitched squeak, I saw Ian's face appear over her shoulder. She turned to kiss him, murmured that it was his turn, and they both sunk out of view. A few minutes later, I was treated to his long, low moan.

After that first event, I heard or saw other couplings over the following couple of weeks. I watched him eat her pussy one night while she reclined on a chaise lounge—although it's entirely possible he was massaging her thighs while nuzzling her navel. I saw her blow him on their living room sofa—or maybe she merely fell asleep on his lap. I caught him finger-fucking her on the sofa—although I suppose he could have caught his thumb in the zipper of her jeans. I observed her stroking him off in the bath—or maybe she was just making sure his dick was really, really clean.

All of this made it harder for me to maintain my stoic quest to become the Responsible Adult Woman I wanted to be. Instead of searching the real estate ads for a place I could afford, instead of pounding out three hundred words a day on my novel, instead of signing up for speed-dating at the local coffee shop, I found myself staring into space, wondering what was going on next door. I couldn't sleep, became restless, and eventually resorted to that old standby, masturbation.

At first, I worked it into my schedule on the Blackberry. I allotted five minutes for a morning rub. Then I gave in and allowed myself not only a morning rub, but also an evening hump with a favorite pillow between my legs. After a while, I scheduled a noon-er with my Rabbit every other day.

Instead of becoming dry and organized, my already messy life got wetter and stickier.

Then this last event occurred. The one that sent me over the fucking edge.

The other morning—or night, depending on how you look at it—I was rising to start my day just as Ian and Susan were returning home from a night on the town. I heard the throaty roar of Ian's BMW as he wedged into a parking spot across the street. I watched him come around and open the door for Susan. As I stood in the darkness in my panties and T, I couldn't help but notice her long, tanned legs slide off the leather seat as she slid into his arms for a lingering kiss.

While I made coffee in the subtle glow of a nightlight, my eyes followed them. Because our houses were on a hill, their first-floor bedroom sat opposite my second-floor kitchen and dining room. Their flimsy curtains were drawn, but did little to prevent me from seeing Ian usher Susan inside and push her onto the bed. Because the weather was mild, windows were open and I could make out the rustle of sheets and Susan's sigh. I sat the canister of coffee aside and retreated into darkness.

Susan wore a short, low-cut black dress and heels. Ian was smartly dressed in black slacks and a green V-neck sweater. From all appearances, they'd just returned from an evening of clubbing. He stood before Susan, his crotch level with her face as she sat on the bed. She reached for his belt buckle and started to unzip his fly, but he pushed her hands away. I heard him ask her if she'd enjoyed herself that evening.

To which she replied, "God yes."

Then he said he wanted her to show him.

Obediently, Susan turned, positioned herself on all fours and pulled her dress up over her hips. She was facing me, so I was denied a good look at her behind, but I was imagining it in all its glory. I caught a flash of black thong riding up her lower back and could see the expression on her face. She was aroused, biting her lower lip and flushed. Ian knelt on his hands and knees and leaned in for a closer look.

"Yes," he said. "I can see you really liked that other couple."

"I soaked myself," she admitted.

Ian lifted a hand to her ass and caressed it. Then he pulled the wisp of a thong aside to allow for closer inspection.

"Oh yeah, Susan, you're dripping."

"Yes, yes I am."

"Who did you like best at the club, Roger or Heather?"

"Both. I liked them both. I liked Roger's body when we danced. He was kind of roly-poly—soft, not hard and lean like you. And I liked the way Heather touched me."

Ian's eyes appeared far away. His left hand rested on Susan's buttock. His right hand was moving, circling and dipping. I imagined him plying the deep furrow between his wife's legs, entering her with a finger, swirling juices over her clit.

"She touched you under the table, didn't she?" he inquired.

"Yes," Susan gasped, "like you're doing now."

She began to rock on the bed, and I became aware that my left hand was cupping and squeezing my right breast through my T while my right hand sought entry down the front of my white cotton panties.

Ian's voice grew harsher, deeper. The expression on his face changed. His eyebrows narrowed; his lips pursed.

"You're a naughty girl, aren't you, Susan? Rubbing up against Roger. You think I didn't see that? Spreading your legs for Heather. You think I didn't know?"

"I couldn't help myself."

"You touched his cock, didn't you?"

"Yes," Susan confessed. "In the bathroom, I stroked it."

"You sucked him off, didn't you, you dirty little cunt? You sucked him off on your hands and knees in the toilet?"

"Yes, fuck yes."

By now, my left hand was pinching a firmed-up nipple through my T and the fingers of my right hand were sliding past the patch of black fur that guarded my pussy. I parted my labia and dipped an index finger into my opening. My backside thumped against the polished stainless steel of the refrigerator.

My eyes were glued to Ian as he removed his shirt. His chest was hairless. He was slender but muscular, his muscles like cabled wire. He twisted the shirt into a rope and drew back his arm. In one swift motion, he delivered a crisp, stinging smack to Susan's bottom. My ass twitched as if it had been struck.

"Ooooh," she squealed.

"You're such a slut."

"I'm sorry. I've really been a bad girl."

The tip of the shirt danced like a whip on her buttocks and between her cheeks. It grazed her exposed pussy. Her cries revealed a woman in that no-man's zone between pleasure and pain.

I pushed my middle finger deeper and pumped in and out. My left hand slithered under my T and caressed my achy breasts.

Ian laid the shirt on the bed. He shed his trousers and underwear. I got a glimpse of his cock, swollen and red, and his sack, full and swaying, before he pressed his pelvis against Susan's ass. He grabbed a handful of her blonde hair and gave it a yank. She yelped like a smitten puppy. He leaned in close, his face against hers, his lips against her ear.

I heard him whisper, "Did you swallow his cum, you slut?"

"Fuck yes," she grunted out.

Her insolence earned her another shot to her butt cheeks. The sound ricocheted into the night. She yelped again and I stepped out of my sticky panties. I bent over the counter now and would have given just about anything for something stinging on my ass.

There it was—a Teflon spatula.

Ian pushed Susan's face into the bed. Her mouth contorted; drool ran down her chin. I watched as he positioned himself and pushed inside her pussy. Her eyes rolled back in her head and I smacked my ass with that spatula.

Ian fucked her deliberately. He stopped in mid-stroke, leaned over, and whispered again.

"You let Heather finger you, didn't you?"

"God yes."

"How many fingers?"

"Two."

"Just two?"

"Three. Okay? Three fingers."

"She fisted you, didn't she, you slut?"

"Yes, yes, she did. And it was good, so good."

Ian smacked her ass again and she whimpered into the sheets.

I drew my Teflon spatula back and smacked myself hard. Pussy nectar dribbled down my thighs.

Susan made these little mewing sounds as Ian fucked her. His breathing quickened. My Teflon spatula had a ridged, easy-grip end. As I watched their bodies move in concert, I rubbed the notches along the valley of my slit. Judging from the expression on Susan's face, she was nearing her climax. Her eyes closed tight, her mouth opened, the veins in her forehead showed. But Ian wasn't letting her off that easily. He ceased his thrusting and I heard him hiss.

"Did you come when Roger shot in your mouth?"

"Yes, in my panties."

"Did you come when Heather fingered you?"

"Yes. I had to bite my hand to keep from screaming."

"You want to come again, don't you?"

"Yes. I want to come on your cock."

But instead of granting her wish, Ian pulled out with a soft plop and cracked her ass with his open hand.

"Turn around," he told her. "Show me how bad you want it."

Susan turned in the bed to face him. She reclined on her back and opened her legs. For the first time, I got a good look at her pussy. It was waxed bare beneath her flat belly and glistened in the dim light. Her engorged clit protruded like a tiny finger from its distended hood. A breeze stirred and I detected the scent of her sex, musty as a field of mushrooms.

I bit my lower lip and inserted the smooth, curved end of the spatula inside my folds. I groaned in my throat. As I maneuvered in and out, the ridges teased and tortured my clit.

Susan slid a hand between her legs, obviously intent on finishing herself. But Ian was having none of it. He pushed her hand away, picked up his T-shirt, and stung her breasts with it. Her eyes burned a little brighter than before.

"How bad do you want it, my little slut?" he asked.

Her hips pumped on the bed as she watched him between her knees. He stroked his cock slowly as he awaited her answer. I wanted his cock and I wanted her pussy. I wanted them so badly my knees were shaking. I worked that spatula in and out, up and around. I had to steady myself with a free hand on the counter to keep from collapsing.

"Please," Susan whimpered. "Please let me come, Ian. Please, I can't stand it."

He stung her nipples with the shirt again. Her hips cleared the bed and her thighs shuddered.

"Not yet. I'll tell you when."

He climbed onto the bed next to her, his hard cock within inches of her face. He reached into the drawer of a nightstand and removed an oversized dildo. He lubed it deliberately.

"Lift your legs, bitch," he told Susan.

She did as directed. He teased her clit with the dildo. Susan flattened her hands on the bed and inhaled sharply.

"Please," she begged.

Ian probed her with his left hand and stroked his cock against her lips with his right.

She gasped as he pushed the dildo's tip inside. I gasped, too, when my first come racked my body. My pussy clenched and released, clenched and released. I lost my grip on the spatula and it clattered to the kitchen floor. I winced and retreated into the darkness again. I leaned against the fridge and continued rubbing myself, unable to look away.

"You like this cock, Susan?" Ian smeared her face with pre-cum.

"Please, please." Susan's knees were pulled tight to her chest as the tip of the dildo disappeared into her cunt.

Ian began stroking himself in earnest now. Her tongue flicked at the head of his cock. She fucked and bucked that dildo like a banshee.

Then I saw it on his face. His eyes and mouth opened wide in a low grunt. The veins of his neck protruded. He squirted onto her tongue and cheeks and chin, over and over, thick and white.

She squirmed beneath him, lapping at his semen. Her hands clenched her breasts and squeezed hard. He released his cock and the dildo at the same time. He slid off the bed and sunk into a chair, spent.

Susan lowered her legs to the bed, open, the heels of her feet pressed together.

"Please, baby, please," she begged.

I mouthed the words along with her, "Please, please."

He rolled his eyes and waved a hand dismissively. "Finish yourself," he said.

She propped herself up on one elbow while she pleasured herself with the dildo. I was right there with her, humping my hand. We came together, her head thrown back in a muted scream. I bent double, steadied once again by the kitchen counter, shuddering out an orgasm that buckled my knees.

When I looked up, Susan and Ian were kissing.

"I love you," he told her.

"I love you too, baby," she replied.

When he headed into bathroom, she pulled on a nightgown and cast a look over her shoulder.

Then she winked in my direction.

Or, at least, I thought she did.

Three weeks have passed since that wink.

Or imagined wink.

My life has dissipated into a puddle. I've totally lost it. Unpaid bills and unopened mail litter the kitchen table. My half-finished novel cries out for completion or disposal. I'm inclined to the latter. I lost the Blackberry, stopped running, and dropped out of the Writers' Workshop. I bought a family-sized bag of Snickers and filled the freezer with fucking Fat Boys.

My days and nights blend together. I linger behind curtains and hunker in bushes, hoping for a peek. I peer over countertops and walls.

I wander through my house naked. I masturbate ceaselessly, often on my deck or patio, not caring who sees me grinding on all fours or writhing on my back.

Susan and Ian have also given up any semblance of modesty. They fuck and suck in plain view, behind their four walls. They play their little games with dildos and vibrators and strap-ons. They tie up and tease. They spank and manipulate.

Two months have passed and we've not exchanged a word. What's there to say?

THE WESTERN FRONT

I shot Larry King right between the eyes with Carlisle's Desert Eagle. My neighbor Rusty came over to my mobile home when the blast went off. None of our neighbors at Crestview Estates seemed to notice.

"Nice shot, Jolene," Rusty said through his handlebar mustache.

He was drunker than me, shirtless, and in serious need of a haircut.

"I missed," I told him.

I'd been gunning for that son of a bitch, Dick Cheney, but it was hard enough for a woman my size to hold and shoot a Desert Eagle, much less aim one.

I had it in for Cheney for keeping my Carlisle in Iraq twice as long as he said he would. I had it in for Bush, and Rummy, and Condi too. Cheney just happened to be interviewing on Larry King.

Carlisle was with the 1st Battalion out of Camp Lejeune. They were the baddest-ass marines on the planet, and they were assigned to the baddest-ass place in Iraq—the Anbar province. So, don't get me wrong, I was proud of my Carlisle, but it was time for him to come home.

I figured I might kill someone for real if I didn't get some of Carlisle's special loving soon.

The next morning, I went to see Rusty. The remains of my TV lay scattered throughout my trailer like pieces of a Humvee hit by an IED.

"You want me to build you a what?" Rusty's eyes looked like ten miles of bad road.

I invited myself inside his trailer and spread my plans across his kitchen table. I'd gotten up early to work on them.

"A spanking machine," I told him.

"You mean as in whup your ass, spanking?"

"That's right."

Rusty was an old jarhead himself, a Vietnam veteran. When he wasn't drinking, he operated the best handyman business in Onslow County.

"Well, Jo," he said, "I'll whup your ass."

"This ass belongs to Carlisle."

Rusty was thirty years older than me and knew where we stood. He'd appeared on my doorstep two days after Carlisle deployed. He acknowledged that I was Carlisle's new wife and all, then offered to fuck me every once in a while in Carlisle's absence so I wouldn't be tempted to step out on my man. He considered it a patriotic gesture. I'd told him no thanks, but said we could be drinking buddies.

We howled at the moon a couple of times a week.

After studying my plan, he said, "I don't think this'll work. You got yer gizmo where yer jimmerjammer should be."

"Well, can you build me a spanking machine, or not?"

"You're goddamn right I can, but it won't look like this."

"How much you want to build it?"

"Your money's no good with me."

"How 'bout I cover materials and buy you a case?"

"Carolina Blonde?"

"Yep."

"You got a deal."

We shook on it.

Five days a week, I waitressed at the M-16 Diner on Topsail Island. It wasn't bad, if you didn't count the toxic level of lard exposure and the guys hitting on you. Anyway, it was only temporary. Carlisle and I had plans to move to Colorado and open our own diner—about as far away from North Carolina, the Marines, and hurricanes as we could get.

That evening, I came home, stacked large pieces of my TV in a wheelbarrow, and carted them to the Dumpster. Rusty's pickup was nowhere in sight.

I figured it was a good time to rub one out for Carlisle.

I started with a hot bath before setting up the video cam and tripod. I pulled the shades, lit candles, and turned back the covers. I took out the dildo I kept in the drawer of the nightstand. It was an exact replica of Carlisle's cock, all the way down to the veins along the shaft and the ridge left over from his circumcision. We'd had it made in Raleigh just before he shipped out. Behind a curtain that barely hid us from view, I'd taken him in my mouth. When he was hard, a plaster cast was set. From the plaster cast, a woman with tattoos and piercings created the dildo.

I got on my hands and knees, stuck my ass in the air, and flipped on the video cam with the remote. I spoke into the headset that held the microphone, "Video #272."

I tugged the flyswatter out from under the mattress. I reached behind and caressed my butt.

"Hey, Carlisle, I'm missing you again tonight," I whispered into the mike.

I ran the flyswatter over my bottom while teasing my slit with the dildo. I bumped and humped like a stripper. I peeked at the camera from under my armpit.

"I was thinking about how you like to take me over your knee, just like Daddy, when I'm a bad girl. That's a good game, isn't it?"

I did my best to swat myself. It was a little awkward, which is why I needed that spanking machine.

"I was thinking about how you like me to assume the position, sergeant. I've been a naughty little private, haven't I?"

I rubbed the dildo against my clit. I was as wet as a leaky faucet.

"Or maybe, Preacher Carlisle, I've been teasing you while you've been trying to save my soul. I'm so bad."

I swatted again and felt the endorphins kick in.

"I was thinking about how you like to lift my skirt over my hips, yank my panties down to my ankles, and paddle me with the palm of your hand."

I pushed the head of the dildo between my pussy lips. I gasped and fought to slow myself down.

"And after you warm me up, I love the way you finger-fuck me, Carlisle. You know, bring me to the edge, back off, then spank me some more."

I punctuated these last few words with more swats. With practice, I'd gotten so I could deliver some pretty good blows.

"I can feel your cock pressing against my belly, Carlisle, as I squirm on your lap. I know you'll give it to me eventually. You'll give it to my mouth, my tits, my pussy, or my ass—wherever you want. Yeah, baby, you'll give it to me."

With those last words, I plunged the dildo deep inside and groaned like a construction worker swinging a hammer. I zoomed in with the remote. I wanted Carlisle to see my reddened cheeks and the wink of my asshole. I wanted him to see the way my pussy gripped his cock.

"Oh, Carlisle," I said, "fill me up, baby."

I rocked and bounced. I turned up the volume so he could hear the squish I made as I closed in on my come.

Just before it hit, I glanced over my shoulder, cooing for the camera, "Can I come, baby? Please, let me come. Please, Carlisle, please."

I could imagine his bass drawl across the miles. *Go for it, girl. Come on Daddy's big cock.*

I sat back and ground out an ass-twitching, thigh-shuddering, belly-clenching, top-of-the-lungs-screaming, bitch-in-heat orgasm. It left me face-down and panting.

The dildo slipped out with a soft plop.

I turned and faced the camera. I squeezed my 36Cs, milking the nipples. "Now, shoot on my titties, Carlisle. That's it, shoot your man-juice all over me."

I closed my eyes and gave him my best "fuck me" face. I imagined him standing there stroking off. I imagined the slip and the slide, the blur of his hand. I could almost feel him hot and creamy on my skin.

"That's it, baby. That's it. Give it to your girl."

I was about to go for another round when I heard banging at my door. I kissed the camera, told Carlisle how much I loved him, and signed off from "The Western Front."

I pulled on my jeans, slipped a T-shirt over my head, and padded through my trailer.

My nipples were still hard from fucking Carlisle and Rusty's eyes locked on to them the moment I flung the door open. He leaned against the railing, a toothpick jutting from one side of his mouth.

"You all right?" he asked.

"How long you been standing here?"

"Long enough to hear you carryin' on."

"I stubbed my toe."

He shifted the toothpick to the other side of his mouth. "Whatever."

"So, what can I do for you, Rusty?"

"I went to the junkyard. Picked up some parts for your machine. I thought you might want to see."

"Let me get my shoes."

His truck was loaded down. There was an electric motor that weighed about three tons, a couple of old bicycles, rusted bed springs, shafts, cranks, and widgets you wouldn't believe.

"The commode's for me," Rusty explained. "Man can always use a spare."

"Impressive."

"I figure to hook up the electric motor to those bicycle wheels, then adjust the tension with a gadget. We can use the bedsprings . . ."

"I don't need the details. I just need to know how long."

"A few days."

"The sooner the better."

We unloaded the pickup into Rusty's workshop. It was high Carolina summer, hot and humid enough to drown flies. After unloading, we dragged a spare window air conditioner into the yard, plugged it in using a long, orange extension cord, and set up a couple of lawn chairs. We positioned a twelve-pack between us.

After a couple of beers, I went inside and microwaved a pizza. After a couple of more beers, along about firefly time, Rusty asked if Carlisle and I were into that kinky shit.

"Depends on what you mean by kinky."

His eyes narrowed to slits and the smoke curled above his head like a serpent set to strike. "You know, tying up. Whips and chains and such. It's un-American."

"We're not into the lifestyle," I explained. "We just like to play games."

"Games?"

"It gets me all worked up."

He blew three smoke rings and considered what I'd said. "How'd y'all get into that?"

"Just messin' around. We didn't know we'd like it so much until we gave it a try."

Rusty flicked his cigarette butt into the parking lot. Sparks flew. "Damn, honey."

"Anyway, it's none of your business."

"I'll work on that machine first thing in the morning."

I kissed him on the cheek and weaved back home. Just before turning in, I uploaded video clip #272 to the website I'd set up. Carlisle's password allowed him to watch and wank to his heart's content.

I opened the curtain and peeked out. Rusty was just finishing the twelve-pack. He cast a lingering look at my trailer before plodding inside.

He forgot to turn off the air conditioner and it cooled the mosquitoes all night long.

Days passed. Every evening, I'd check Rusty's progress.

"Not yet," he'd growl.

I'd wake in the middle of the night and hear banging, drilling, and sawing. Once, I saw the flash of welding.

To pass the time, I made videos #273 through #275.

Then, one morning, a used TV sat on my doorstep with a note from Rusty. He'd made a second trip to the junkyard. The TV was a throw-in from the dealer. The note went on to say that he expected to finish work on the machine by the end of the day.

I hustled tables and slung food in a daze. Eggs and hash browns. Omelets and sandwiches. Cherry pie *à la mode*.

In the dead time between two and five, CNN reported that our third hurricane of the season was forming off the coast. When I left work for the day, I could smell that 'cane brewing to the east, could feel the breeze on my face, could see the chop in the water. Dark clouds lay on the horizon. Hard-bodied boys and girls rode the high surf on Topsail Beach.

Rusty was sitting in the yard with his air conditioner when I pulled up. He was already deep into a twelve-pack of Blonde.

"This one's on the house," he said, handing me a bottle. "You still owe me a case plus materials."

"You finish my machine?"

"Damn straight."

"How's it look?"

"Come on." He led me to his workshop.

It stopped me in my tracks.

He'd built a twelve-by-twelve wooden platform and mounted the damn thing on bedsprings. At the rear of the platform was that electric motor we'd busted a gut unloading from his pickup. Attached to the motor was a rod that led to two bicycle wheels. The wheels drove a piston with an arm. Sprockets and springs dangled. The end of the arm was fitted with a ping-pong paddle. In front of the paddle was an old vaulting horse with stirrups bolted on the sides and handles for holding on to. A faux fur saddle stretched across the top.

"Whaddaya think?" he asked.

"Jesus Christ."

"It's somethin', ain't it?"

"Jesus Fucking Christ."

"You like it?"

I sat my beer down on top of a table covered with dust, bug carcasses, and discarded nuts and bolts. Hands on my hips, I turned on him. "What the fuck, Rusty? This'll never fit in my trailer."

He looked like he'd been kicked in the balls. "Yer trailer?"

"You think I want to traipse over here every time I want my hind end lit up?"

He frowned. "I didn't know you wanted a portable machine."

I walked around it. He'd put in a lot of effort. His craftsmanship was obvious.

"Does it work?" I ran my fingers over the scratchy surface of the ping-pong paddle.

Rusty approached a control panel. He flipped a switch and it lit up like a Christmas tree. "Goddamn right, it works. We need to test for pressure and fit, but she hammers away pretty good."

"Pressure and fit?"

"You can calibrate the height of the saddle here and the strike force there." He made pointing motions.

"I see."

"And the horse is mounted on rails, so you can adjust the distance from the paddle."

"Okay."

"The electric motor is hooked up to a generator, which allows for usage even in the event of a power outage."

Outside, the sky was turning green.

I touched the faux fur. "Where'd you get this?"

"The pawn shop. The horse vibrates too. It's optional."

"Vibrates?"

"Three different speeds. Remember those vibrating beds in cheap hotels?"

I didn't have the heart to tell him that was before my time.

"Whaddaya think?" he asked. "Aside from the size?"

"Aside from the size, it's damned impressive."

His eyes lit up. "I may be able to miniaturize, but we should try her out before I make adjustments."

"Try her out?"

"A test drive."

"Well, I see your point."

"I'll show you how to operate it. Once you're in the saddle, the control panel is within reach."

"All right. Let's give her a go." I was still dressed in my waitress uniform, but I put one foot in the stirrup and threw the other over the horse.

I hiked up my skirt, positioned my heinie, and grabbed hold. Rusty pushed a button and that big electric motor commenced to hum. The bicycle wheels squeaked into action. The arm swung and I felt the pop of that paddle to the bone.

"Might want to turn her down a notch," I hollered over the racket.

Rusty cranked a dial. He lowered the front end of the horse for a better angle.

Whack! That sumbitch caught me again.

"What speed?" he shouted.

"Every fifteen, twenty seconds. Can you make her switch from one bun to the other?"

"Hell, yeah." He came around behind me. "I just need to loosen this thingamajig."

Pop!

"That's better."

"I like yer pink thong. You want to try the vibrator?"

Smack!

"Sure, might as well."

Rusty turned another dial. "High or low?"

Crack!

"Right there."

That horse thrummed between my legs like a Harley.

"Mind if I sit?" Rusty pulled up a chair.

Whack!

"Make yourself comfortable." I readjusted the dial for more pressure and faster strokes.

I squeezed my eyes shut and thought about Carlisle, his firm hand and sure touch. I thought about how he could lift me up and bring me down. I thought about his broad chest and hard abs, his strong thighs and stiff cock. I gripped that horse a little harder with my thighs.

Whap!

Suddenly, I felt flushed and drippy, breathy and lost in the moment. It was more than I'd counted on. I was about to explode.

"All right, that's enough. Time to turn this thing off, Rusty." I sounded calmer than I was.

He was on his feet, a concerned look on his face. "Hold on."

Kapow!

"I said turn this damn thing off."

"Hold on, the whammerjammer's stuck on the dingaling."

Unlike Carlisle, that machine didn't know when to let up or stop. My ass was on fire, my pussy aglow.

"Rusty . . ."

He had a plumber's wrench in his hand. He swore and delivered a clanking blow.

But I'd reached a place with only one exit. I ground my pelvis into the thrum and howled.

Just then, the machine chugged to a halt. I collapsed, moaning as the aftershocks coursed through my body. It didn't satisfy. It just left me wanting more.

"You all right?" Rusty asked.

"No, I'm not all right. I'm a fuckin' mess."

He stood in front of me, a big old boner tenting his jeans. "Sorry," he said.

"You shouldn't be sorry."

I slid off the horse, loose in the belly and weak in the knees.

He took my hand and I stepped into his embrace. "I was just tryin' to help."

"Oh, Rusty, I miss my man."

"I know, honey," he said.

He was beery and sweaty and hard as a tire iron. I loved Carlisle and all, but damn, it felt good to be held. The bulge behind Rusty's zipper twitched.

I ground my pelvis against his. I kissed him on the neck and whispered, "I could help you with that, Rusty."

He went tense all over. "I thought we had an arrangement."

"I could make an exception."

I dropped to the floor. I unzipped Rusty's jeans and unfurled his hard-on.

"Jo, you don't need to . . ."

"Oh, yes I do."

He tasted like a man, not a silicone dildo. It had been six months since I'd had that taste. I bobbed and swirled, licked and sucked.

Rusty gazed down at me like I was an angel.

I stood, turned, and lifted my waitress uniform over my head. I bent over that horse. "You got a . . ."

He dug in his wallet. I heard the crinkle of a wrapper. "You sure about this?"

"Just shut up and fuck me."

He was thicker than Carlisle, but had a soft touch for a big man.

"Yer ass is as red as an apple," he said.

"You can slap it if you want."

"You sure?"

"Goddamnit, Rusty, slap my ass."

All night, rain fell in sheets. By morning, water rose in the fields. Channel 10 News advised evacuation. Rusty and I holed up in a motel on the interstate for three days.

There wasn't any kind of love we didn't make. I guess we were both starved for it. He proved to be a kind and gentle lover, too kind and gentle for me. But I wasn't looking for a lover, just a port in the storm.

I explained to him that this was a one-time deal, and if he ever brought it up again or said a word to Carlisle, I'd blow his head off with that Desert Eagle. He said he had no doubts.

A week later, Carlisle called. The good news was he was leaving Iraq. The bad news was he'd been redeployed to Afghanistan—ninety more days chasing ghosts in the thin, dry air.

"You okay?" I asked.

"Just keep those clips coming. How 'bout you?"

"All's quiet on the Western Front."

"I miss you, Jolene."

"I'll be right here, baby, waiting for you."

Except I hadn't exactly waited and I'd have to live with that the rest of my life.

That evening, while we sat beneath the stars and drank beer, I passed along the news about Carlisle to Rusty. He went on an impassioned rant against the military-industrial complex. Then he opened a couple of more beers.

That's when he laid it on me. He'd decided to leave Caroline for California. Those three days he'd spent with me had convinced him to straighten out, get a real job, and find a good woman of his own.

"I guess that makes you the Western Front," I said.

"What?"

"Inside joke. When're you leaving?"

"Soon as I get packed and we take that machine apart."

I thought about Carlisle's remaining ninety days. It was a long time to go without a spanking.

I patted Rusty on the knee. "Maybe you should leave that machine here," I told him.

TORN IN TWO

I should've been relaxing in front of a roaring fire. Instead, I was standing in a cold house, staring at the corpse of a nude woman whose nipples had been sliced off. Just above where her left nipple should've been, the murderer had left his signature—a tattoo of a heart torn into two jagged pieces.

Lenny Szerbiak, the lead detective on the case, continued to stare at the body as he spoke. "It's a copycat, counselor. It's gotta be."

"Yeah, well, if it's a copycat, why the hell did you call me?"

I couldn't take my eyes off the body either. She was like all the others—blue-eyed and blonde, young and pretty.

"Look, Miss Bartkowski, just because we're on different sides of the aisle doesn't mean I don't respect your work."

"Yeah, right." I kept my bullshit detector on high when it came to cops.

"I'm just sayin', it's got to be a copycat, but I ain't sure it's a copycat."

"Whaddaya mean?"

Lenny motioned for me to follow him. As we stepped into the parking lot, a team of forensics experts pushed past.

"I mean, I know a little about ink. A tattoo artist's work is like a fingerprint. Ain't no two the same."

"So?"

"So, the ink says the guy who killed this broad is the same guy who killed Shana Hellwig."

"Except, last I heard, Armand Heimlich's in prison."

But Lenny knew that; he'd been the lead detective on the string of murders that led to Armand's conviction. I knew it because Armand was my client.

"Yeah, well."

Lenny fished a crumpled pack of cigarettes from his parka pocket. He offered me one and I took it—even though I quit three months ago, right after Armand's trial. But I've quit and started a hundred times before. Law school exams, divorces, and murder trials are good for tobacco sales.

"Why don't you admit you fucked up, detective. Armand never committed those other murders. The real Nipplelicious Murderer is still out there. This is proof."

Lenny blew smoke out of his nostrils. "This ain't proof of shit, counselor. You know as well as I do the DNA don't lie. That was Armand's DNA under Shana Hellwig's fingernails."

Shana Hellwig was the last of seven women Armand Heimlich was charged with killing. The modus operandi was the same in every instance: nipples missing; tattoo applied; cause of death, asphyxiation. There was no sign of forced entry, no trace of the killer's bodily fluids, and no indication of a struggle—except in Shana's case. She'd fought for her life.

"So, where does this leave us?"

Lenny tossed his cigarette into a bank of ugly, gray snow. "Beats the fuck outta me."

He was a good-looking man with gray-flecked hair, a square jaw, and thick, sensual lips. I guessed he was in his late forties. He was a big guy, tall and muscular. A man's man. My kinda man.

"Yeah, Lenny, I know what you mean."

"Anyways," he said, "I'll keep you in the loop."

I took a last drag on my cigarette. Maybe Lenny's good looks shorted out my bullshit detector.

"Whaddaya doing for Christmas dinner?" I asked.

"Not much. Watchin' the football game and hangin' with the guys."

I'd read it right. He was divorced, like me. Alone and able to handle it if he had to, like me.

"Why don't you come over to my place? I've got plenty enough for two."

He jammed his hands into his jeans pockets. "You cook, counselor?"

He didn't know the half of it.

"Come on," I said. "I've got a place in Shorewood."

The snow started with big fluffy flakes, then turned to wind-driven pellets. I didn't need a weatherman to tell me we were in for it.

I opened a bottle of Zinfandel. "How about a glass of wine?"

"I'm usually a beer guy, but I can make an exception."

I swirled the dark red liquid and inhaled the scent of black cherry, pepper, and currant. "Sorry, I don't keep beer in the house."

Lenny gave the wine a try, then nodded. "This'll work."

My chef's knife flashed under the fluorescent light as I made a *mirepoix* of onions, carrots, and bell pepper.

"I think you've done this before," he said.

"I went to law school in New Orleans. I worked the restaurants there to make a few extra bucks. By the time I graduated, I was a line cook at Nola."

"I'm impressed."

"You do what you have to do."

I stirred the *mirepoix* in a heavy pot. When the vegetables caramelized, I transferred them to a bowl and went to work on the *roux*. I let the *roux* cook until it turned mahogany in color, then returned the vegetables to the pot. I seasoned the mixture with my secret combination of Cajun spices.

Lenny breathed in deeply through his nostrils. "That smells incredible."

"I hope you don't mind spicy."

"The spicier the better."

I filled the pot with chicken stock and chopped *andouille* sausage. I'd wait to add the shrimp until the last three minutes.

"We'll let that simmer for a while," I told him as I assembled two salads of greens and fresh tomatoes. I handed him the bottle of Zin. We needed a refill. "Here, make yourself useful."

I sliced bread, filled a dish for dipping with olive oil, and set the table in the dining room overlooking the cold, gray lake. Lenny poured more wine and lit candles.

"Cheers," I said, raising my glass.

"To the chef."

Shrimp *etouffee*. That's my kind of Christmas dinner.

"So," Lenny said, "after the divorce, she moved to Kenosha with the kids to be closer to her family."

I watched him load up another forkful of *etouffee* and shovel it in. He was on his second helping and still going strong. I was used to feeding people who were concerned with their weight. Feeding a man who was big and hungry and ate with such relish was a welcome change.

"But you stayed here to save the world from crime?"

He reached for the wine bottle and split the remainder between us. Sure enough, we'd killed that first bottle.

"The thing is, I'm pushing fifty and there are only a couple of things I've ever been good at in life. One of them is police work. The other, well . . . Anyway, I'm still here."

He looked younger, softer—warmer—in the candle light. I hoped I did too.

"Well, I'm glad you are," I said.

He looked up. "So am I."

It was cold, but the snow had let up. I wore a cashmere cardigan and an old parka; Lenny was in the sweatshirt and down vest he'd worn at the crime scene earlier in the day. We walked through Lake Park. Snow clung to the trees, giving them an unworldly appearance. A half moon peeked through the clouds and illuminated the lake.

"So, if most of your clients are guilty, why do you do it?" he asked.

"I started doing it to make a living. Anymore, I do it for the same reason you do police work—I can't see myself doing anything else and I'm good at it."

"You're damn good, that's for sure."

A sudden and unexpectedly strong gust of wind buffeted us. "I'm freezing," I said.

"C'mon, we better get back."

He slid an arm around my waist. I didn't resist the urge to lean against him, my hip pressed to his. We walked that way to my place without speaking. At the door, we stood in the yellow porch light. I looked up at him.

"I feel like a high school kid," he said.

"We're not kids, Lenny."

"No, I guess we're not."

"I really enjoyed this evening," I told him. Maybe it was the wine talking, but I meant what I said.

He jammed his hands in his pockets and stared at his boots. "Yeah, Cindy, me too."

"So, are you going to kiss me good night or not?"

He took my face in his hands and brought his mouth to mine. "Yeah, I'd like that."

We barely made it into the foyer before I backed him against a wall. Our tongues swirled and darted. I felt his hands slide down my back and over the curve of my hips. I fumbled with the buttons on his shirt. His lips were hot and damp on my ears and neck.

"Lenny," I whispered into the mat of hair on his chest.

He emitted a scent of male musk I hadn't encountered in a while. I felt my sweater and blouse fall to the floor. He expertly unhooked my bra and pushed it off my shoulders. We both watched my white breasts spill into his waiting hands. I ran my fingers through his hair.

Then, that quick, he spun me around. My face pressed against the wall and his pelvis was hard on my ass. He unbuttoned my jeans and tugged them off my hips. I stepped clear of the denim. In one swift motion, he pulled my undies to the ground.

"Fuck yeah." I didn't mean to say it, but I meant what I said.

I searched behind me and loosened his belt buckle. I needed his cock in my hand, needed to feel it throb and ache.

He groaned when I stroked the length and thickness of it. I used my thumb to spread the dew that gathered at the tip. I reached lower and cupped his soft, furry balls in my palm.

He stepped away and I turned to face him again. He shucked his jeans and boxers, and I saw him naked for the first time. I took it all in—the wide shoulders and bulging arms, the virile chest, the swaying hard-on, the muscular buttocks and legs. I steered him into my bedroom and pushed him onto the bed. I threw a leg over him, straddling his belly.

He looked up, face red, breath short. "I've wanted you since the first time I saw you in that courtroom."

I leaned forward to plant a kiss on his lips. "Yeah, you wanted me that long?" I brushed my nipples against his, teasing him.

"Yeah, that long."

He reached for me, but I pinned his arms to the bed and lowered my breasts to his face, purring and rubbing like a cat.

Then I took his hand and guided it between my legs. He looked up, his eyes bright with desire. "You wanted this that first day in court?"

"Yeah, I wanted your pussy."

His fingers opened me, dipped into my slit, and drew moisture. His eyes never left mine as he explored the folds and valleys until I cried out.

"Oh, baby," I murmured.

I meant to ride him—I always came like that—but he had other ideas. He sat up and turned me over. He was strong enough that I couldn't have resisted even if I'd wanted to. He positioned me on my hands and knees and pushed my face into the sheets, my ass and cunt exposed and ready for the taking. He rubbed his cock between my ass cheeks, like a hot dog in a bun. Every time he grazed my asshole, my thighs clenched. Then he opened me and pushed between my pussy lips, giving me his head.

"That's it," I said.

"There's more where that came from."

I tried to push against him, but his hand on the small of my back prevented it.

"Give it all to me. Give me that cock." It sounded needier than I'd intended.

He pushed a little deeper and I tightened around him. "You're so wet," he said.

"Damn," I groaned.

Then he slammed into me hard, crashing into my cervix and driving the breath out of me.

He pulled out and drove in hard again. I barked like a bitch in heat.

Then he found his rhythm, in and out. I howled. He grunted. Face hard against the bed, I reached between my legs, found my clit, and stroked one, two, three times. That was all it took. One after another, the waves pulsed through me. I shuddered and cried out.

Lenny wasn't far behind. I felt him shoot inside me, his cock buried deep.

I collapsed, panting. He rolled off and lay beside me.

He turned his head and winked. "That work for you?"

"What do you think?"

"I think you fuck like an animal."

I took it as a compliment and reached out and squeezed his arm. "Yeah, and you made me."

Afterwards, we sat in front of the fire, sipping Bailey's and filling gaps. I counted it in his favor when I asked him to stay over and he said he'd like that. I went to sleep in his arms, his lips whispering good night, his cock pressed into the crack of my ass. I figured a girl could do a lot worse.

It was when I woke from a dead sleep that things got funky.

I lay on my back, spread-eagled. My hands were cuffed to the bed post. My feet were secured to the foot of the bed with pantyhose. Lenny sat next to me in the near dark, his left hand playing from one of my breasts to the other.

"Lenny, what the fuck?"

He pinched my left nipple and my hips cleared the bed. "C'mon, you like it, right?"

My mouth was dry, my head a little achy. "Yeah, I like it all right."

He pinched my right nipple and I squirmed. He reached out and, in the moonlight, stretched a gossamer string of pre-cum from his pee-hole to my tongue. I licked and sucked like a child with an ice cream cone.

"Yeah, you like it."

He repositioned and sat over me, his cock fat and slippery between my breasts. He tugged at each nipple, gently at first, then harder.

I made a sound like a construction worker swinging a sledge hammer.

He smiled and thrust between my tits. I felt the drag of his balls across my belly, felt the tip of his cock bump my chin. My ass clenched and my hips cleared the bed again.

He twisted my nipples. I closed my eyes and went with it. I'd be sore tomorrow, but there was no stopping tonight. He reached between my thighs. Two fingers entered and probed. He brought his fingers to my face. They smelled of sex. I licked again.

"Yeah," he said, "you really like it. See how wet you are?"

"Fuck me, Lenny. C'mon, fuck me."

"I'm gonna fuck you my way," he told me.

He leaned across the bed and fumbled through the clothes he'd left draped over a chair. From his jacket, he produced a chain. I heard its clink, then felt the cold metallic bite of nipple clamps.

"What the . . ."

He draped the chain around his neck and sat upright. I yelped and arched my back, struggling against the cuffs and ties. My nipples screamed with pleasure and pain. My pussy was on fire.

He lowered his face to my ear. "Too much?"

"No," I managed.

"You're a real slut, aren't you, counselor?"

He'd seen through the veneer of respectability right to the heart of the easiest girl at Tulane Law. "Yeah, baby, I'm your slut."

He sat up again, sending a lightning bolt of pleasure and pain through my nipples, and began moving in earnest. With each thrust forward, I extended my tongue, trying to lick his cockhead. With each retreat, my nipples reached a new level of sweet agony.

Lenny's breathing grew more rapid. My hips and legs thrashed against the sheets. He slowed and took his cock in his hand. I opened my mouth in anticipation, watching him stroke, waiting for my reward. Finally, he bucked, spraying my lips, cheeks, chin, and breasts with his cream. I lapped at him like a woman dying of thirst. When his ejaculations ceased, I sucked him until he went flaccid in my mouth.

Finally, he withdrew and loosened the clamps. He rolled off me and unclasped the cuffs.

"Finish yourself," he said.

I was overcome with lust, swollen and dripping. I watched him dry his cock with Kleenex and I reached for my cunt. He pulled on his jeans and shirt while I circled and dipped. He tied his shoes while I fingered deep and hard, and ground the palm of my hand against my clit.

My free hand reached out for him. "Oh . . ."

I came like thunder on the fucking prairie.

As he walked out the door, I came again.

Over the course of the next week, two more women were murdered. True to his word, Lenny invited me to the crime scenes. We stood next to each other and examined the corpses of blue-eyed, blonde-haired women—women I looked like when I was twenty. Women with firm tits, tight asses, and abs like washboards. Except, these were women with their nipples removed, women inked with that damn tattoo.

Lenny invited me to the crime scenes, all right, but the son of a bitch never said a word about the night we spent together. He never sent flowers. He never sent a card. He didn't even call drunk looking for a repeat. The motherfucker acted like nothing had happened.

The third time he summoned me, I was ready for him.

The woman was in her home in Wauwatosa, a cozy suburb near the West Side. Coworkers grew suspicious when she didn't show or call in sick. A nosy neighbor broke in through the back door and found Whitney Beranek in the bedroom. Her eyes were still open. The skin on her breasts, near where her nipples should have been, was an ugly yellow and purple.

"Same old shit," Lenny said. "The profiler figures our killer for a middle-aged white male. That's about half of everyone left in Milwaukee."

"We need to talk, Szerbiak."

Outside, a group of neighbors gathered in the street. Snow three feet deep lay piled at the curb. The bitter January cold pinched my nostrils and made it difficult to breath.

"Why are you doing this, Lenny?"

"Doing what?"

"I think you know."

"I told you I'd keep you in the loop."

"That was before you fucked me. Why have our only dates since then been in the company of mutilated corpses?"

Lenny dug out his cigarettes and offered me one. This time, I declined.

"I didn't think we hit it off all that well," he said.

"Really? You seemed to like it well enough when you were grinding away on top of me."

He shrugged. "Yeah, well."

"I don't go to bed with just anyone." Well, at least not everyone.

"Whatever you say, counselor."

I was so pissed I could've kicked him with my sharp-toed heels. "You know what, Szerbiak?"

"What's that, counselor?"

"Fuck you."

I was more convinced than ever that Armand Heimlich was an innocent man. Whoever was on this current killing spree was the same man who had killed the women Armand had been convicted of killing. The DNA didn't lie, but neither did the ink. And neither did my gut. But it would take more than ink and my gut to get Armand out of jail.

I drove to Waupun Prison to see him. Waupun sat on the edge of Horicon Marsh. In the spring and fall, it was a stopover for Canadian Geese on their semi-annual migration. In the deep winter of late January in Wisconsin, there was something prehistoric, something Ice Age, about it. It wouldn't have surprised me to see woolly mammoths wandering across the landscape.

If the marsh was bleak, the prison was utterly depressing—a castle of stone surrounded by a barbed wire fence set upon the frozen prairie. Cold in the winter, hot in the summer, it was where the worst of Wisconsin's worst paid their debt to society. Ed Gein, a farmer who haunted rest stops and picnic grounds on rural Wisconsin highways and applied his victim's skin to lampshades and furniture, spent time here. So did Jeffrey Dahmer, the chocolate factory worker who turned young men into sexual zombies by injecting chemicals into their brains before feasting on their organs. On average, it took three convictions to earn your way into Waupun. Once there, the average stay was ten years. The recidivism rate was seventy percent. So much for prison as a vehicle for rehabilitation.

I knew the routine. I showed my ID at the gate and parked in the visitor's lot. Once inside, I slipped off my shoes and gave up my belt to pass through security. I endured the pat down from a bulky female guard who looked like she was packing a strap-on in her pants.

I tried not to give it much thought.

When she was done, the woman punched numbers into a keypad to unlock double doors of glass and steel bars, and led me through a six-by-twelve containment chamber monitored by video cameras. If she were more bored, she couldn't have shown it.

At the far end of the chamber, another set of double doors opened into a short, dark hallway. A male guard on the other side punched another keypad and the double doors slid open. When I stepped through, the doors locked behind me with a clunk and a hiss. I remembered the guard's clipped, bristly hair and pointed fox-like ears from previous visits. He looked me over like I was a bratwurst and beer on a hot day at the ballpark.

I met Armand in the Lawyer's Room, a six-by-nine cell with a metal table and two uncomfortable chairs. Armand was cuffed to the table and two armed guards waited outside the door. There was a panic button underneath on my side of the table.

"Hey, Armand," I said.

"Hey, Miss Bartkowski."

Armand wasn't a bad guy compared to some of my clients. White and middle-aged with flaxen hair and pale blue eyes, he fit Szerbiak's profile like a glove. Still unmarried at age forty-five, he'd lived with his mother, working days at a brewery and nights at a tattoo parlor, before being fingered for the Nipplelicious murders.

At trial, he'd offered an alibi witness and his pastor had described for the jury Armand's good works in the community. His record was clean as a whistle. Except for the DNA he'd apparently left behind under Shana Hellwig's fingernails, the jury would never have convicted him. Lenny Szerbiak had originally focused on Armand because he lived in Shana's neighborhood and worked as an ink artist. Lenny and his partner got Armand to agree to a polygraph and a blood test "to clear his name." He passed the polygraph, but his DNA matched what they'd found at the crime scene.

Bingo! Lenny had his man.

"How goes it, Armand?"

"Not bad, I guess."

Compared to what, I wondered. "Well, I just needed to ask you a couple of questions."

"Is this about my appeal?"

"Not really." Cons are always thinking about their appeals. I didn't tell him that, although I'd filed as a matter of course, our chances of winning were about as good as a fart in a snow storm.

"Okay. Ask away."

"Armand, had you ever met or seen Detective Szerbiak before he arrested you?"

There was a dullness to Armand's responses that made him seem like he could be a serial killer. I was never quite sure what was going on behind the flat expression.

"I seen him in the neighborhood bars. He'd come to the Friday Night Fish Fries at the church."

"The church?" I shouldn't have been surprised. It was a Milwaukee tradition.

"Yeah, my church sold fish fries, all you could eat, on Friday nights. I volunteered on the serving line and I remembered seeing him after he arrested me."

"Really?"

"Yeah, a lot of cops are from the Southside. A lot of cops come to fish fries. It wasn't that big of a deal."

"But you remembered him from the fish fry after he arrested you? You remembered him from the serving line?"

"Well, yeah, but I'd seen him at conferences, and such, before that. I knew he was a cop before he ever arrested me."

"Conferences?"

"Yeah, tattoo conventions and conferences, you know. He used to be in the business. I thought it was kinda funny for a cop, but what the hey?"

"Szerbiak was into tattoos?"

"Yeah, they said he moonlighted at a shop in Kenosha."

"No shit."

"That's what they said."

I'm pushing fifty and there are only a couple of things I've ever been good at in life. One of them is police work. The other, well . . .

The remembered words settled on me like an icy wet blanket.

"Why didn't you ever say anything about this, Armand?"

"You never asked."

It's always the most obvious questions that don't get asked. "I think that's all I really needed, Armand."

"You drove all the way up here just to ask me that?"

"Yeah," I said. "Yeah, I guess I did."

I had to hold on to the chair when I stood, my legs were so weak.

It took three weeks of hard work to lure Lenny Szerbiak back to my place for dinner. I called to apologize for telling him to fuck off. He said he understood. I told him I thought we deserved another chance. He said he wasn't sure. I whispered into the cell phone that I couldn't think of anything but his slick dick between my breasts. He agreed to meet for coffee. I wore a low-cut V-neck sweater and a push-up bra, and squeezed him under the table. From there, we progressed to online chatting and a round of phone sex. I knew I had him when I e-mailed a pic of my nipples pinched by clothespins and he followed up with a shot of a woman's wrist cuffed to a bedpost.

While we did our little dance, three more women died. Since our tiff in Wauwatosa, Lenny no longer invited me to the crime scenes, so I read about it in the paper. Carol Slovinsky they found in an apartment in Brown Deer, Debbie Nieman in a townhouse in Glenview, and Sheila Muesenhoffer tied to a La-Z-Boy in her suite at the Pfister Hotel. The pressure was growing on Lenny and his dedicated team to nail the killer—dubbed, logically enough, the Nipplelicious Copycat by the local media. The mayor held a press conference and said there would be no vacations until the "heartless fiend was brought to justice."

In most places, the end of February signaled the end of winter. But in Milwaukee, the end of February was only the beginning of the last three months of winter. The Friday night Lenny appeared at my door with a bouquet of roses and a haircut, snow was falling wet and heavy. By morning, it would be a slushy mess or a frozen wasteland, depending on the temps.

"I can't stay," he said. "I've only got a few hours off with this killer on the loose."

"I'm just glad you're here."

I poured us cabernet and asked him to take a seat at the bar while I finished prepping dinner. My knife chopped and diced. I wore a tight-fitting black wool sweater, a gray mini-skirt, and five-inch hooker heels. Underneath, I'd skipped the bra and panties, opting instead for fishnet thigh-highs.

"So, how's that investigation going?"

"Same old, same old."

"You still convinced it's a copycat?"

"Not a doubt in my mind, counselor."

I seasoned a couple of juicy T-bones and assembled a potato gratin dish my grandma taught me how to make.

"It's a funny thing, though," I said without looking up.

"What's that?"

"I've got family in Chicago. My brother's an ex-cop. He does PI work these days."

"Yeah?"

"He told me that while Armand's trial was going on and the murders stopped here, they had a couple of murders down there. Same titty play, same tattoo. Then once Armand's locked up, the murders stop there, but start again here."

"We're aware of the murders in Chi-town."

I refilled his wine glass. "I figured you were."

My brother told me a few other things. His investigation into Lenny Szerbiak revealed a man with a troubled youth and a marginal adulthood. He grew up in the rough, working-class south side of Milwaukee. Lenny's teachers remembered a pudgy boy who the children teased for having breasts like a girl. On the one hand, a teenage Lenny sang in the church choir. On the other, he spent time in reform school for vandalism and fighting. After high school, he joined the Marines, appeared to clean up his act, and made the police force. But there were rumors of heavy drinking. There was more than the one divorce he told me about. And there were troubling complaints from female officers about a detective who could be overly friendly in tight places.

Lenny sipped his wine and I worked in silence for several minutes. I could feel his eyes all over me and hear the whistle of his breath through his nostrils. When I looked up, Lenny leaned across the bar and kissed me. His face was flushed when he pulled away.

"I gotta have some of you, Cindy. You got me so worked up I can hardly stand it."

I gave him a wicked smile and came around to the other side of the bar. I raised myself up and sat in front of him. My nipples were at eye level. I spread my knees and my skirt slid higher than my thigh-highs. I leaned in and nipped at his ear, pushing my nipples into his face. He lifted the sweater so he could feel skin on skin. I yelped and pulled away when he bit me. Then I whisked off the sweater and sat topless before him.

"You're a titty man, aren't you, Lenny?"

His breathing was quick and shallow, his eyes wide. He swallowed hard. "Always have been."

"Yeah, I thought so."

He lunged and buried his face in my bosom. He slurped and sucked.

"Ooooh, baby," I cooed.

I leaned over and reached into his lap. It felt like he had a tire iron in his pants. I came down off the bar and knelt on the floor. I unzipped him and drizzled saliva on the length of his shaft. I pressed him into the valley between my breasts. I squeezed while he pumped.

"Goddamn," he moaned.

"Fuck my titties, Lenny. That's it, give it to me."

It only took a few strokes to bring him off. It was like a river of goo.

"Shit," he said. "You're something, girl."

Those were his last words before the Rohypnol kicked in. Lenny's eyes rolled back in his head and he toppled off the bar stool, just missing the corner of my coffee table as he fell.

I took my time. I used a syringe to collect his semen and squirted it into a plastic vial. I ran hot water over a dishtowel and cleaned myself. I used Lenny's own cuffs to secure him to my sofa and removed his .38 revolver from his shoulder holster.

Then, I broiled my steak, poured a glass of wine from an untainted bottle, and enjoyed my dinner while Lenny slept it off.

It took him two hours to come around. By the time he did, I'd cleaned up from dinner and changed into jeans and a U of W sweatshirt.

"What the fuck?" he said.

"Over here, Szerbiak."

It took a few moments for his eyes to focus. I sat across from him in my favorite chair.

He broke into a silly grin. "You play rough."

I crawled over to him on my hands and knees. I laid the blade of my chef's knife against his cheek. "Feel cold steel, asshole."

"Jesus Christ, Cindy."

I retreated to my chair. "We can make this easy or hard, Lenny."

"What're you talking about?"

"Your secret's out. I know you're the Nipplelicious Murderer."

"What?"

"You killed the women Armand was convicted of killing. You're a tattoo artist and you left your mark. You thought you might get caught after Shana Hellwig fought you and you were forced to flee the crime scene before you had a chance to clean up. And you were right. It was your skin under her fingernails. But you framed Armand by switching out your DNA for his. It wouldn't have been that hard for the lead detective on the case to gain access to the evidence. Maybe you intended to stop after Armand was arrested, maybe not. But you couldn't. You couldn't even stop while he was on trial. That's why you went down to Chicago. Except you made a mistake down there."

"Yeah? What's that?"

"You left a trace of DNA behind. It must've leaked from your condom, Lenny." I held up my vial. "I'm betting the DNA from Marla Winkelhammer's murder matches this."

The blood drained from his face. He shook his head, started to deny it, then let go. An expression of relief settled over him, but he looked ten years older. "Okay, counselor. What do you want from me?"

"First, I want to know why you didn't kill me."

"Kill you? I never wanted to kill you. I just wanted to tease you."

It made sense. For a serial killer on a power trip, the ultimate trip was teasing the lawyer who'd defended the guy he'd framed for his murders. "That's why you invited me to the crime scenes?"

"It wasn't for your company."

"You really are an asshole, Lenny."

He smiled. "Admit it, counselor, I may be an asshole, but I gave you what you wanted."

For a long moment, I considered shoving my blade into his left eye. Instead, I flipped the switch on the voice recorder I usually used for dictating memos and motions. "Tell me about all those other women, Lenny. The ones that didn't survive."

"You really want to hear."

"Tell it, Lenny. Come to Momma."

That long, cold winter eventually melted into a cool, wet spring. It took that long for the wheels of justice to turn in Lenny's case.

After I got his confession, I gave the tape and the vial to the DA. A genuine prick if there ever was one, Marty Weimereiner refused to stipulate to Armand's innocence at first. It was only when they found the Mason jars on a shelf in a walled-off section of Lenny's basement that Marty came around. Each jar of formaldehyde held a pair of matching nipples. Each jar was labeled with the victim's name.

Lenny hired a friend of mine, Suze Manski, to defend him. He claimed the confession was forced and argued that my method of collecting his DNA violated his civil rights. The judge denied bail and scheduled the trial for late summer.

In the meantime, the killings stopped. That was proof enough of Lenny's guilt for most folks in Milwaukee. That and the Mason jars.

It was late April when I returned to Waupun to meet Armand at the gate, a free man at last. Shoots of green showed through the ice on the marsh. Geese on their way north passed overhead, festooned against the sky in the shape of a boomerang, wings flapping furiously, potbellies sagging, necks extended as they made loud, chaotic honks. Just like in the movies, the sun broke through the clouds and set the puddles of melting snow aglitter as Armand strode to my car.

He waited until he'd settled in the bucket seat next to me to speak. "Miss Bartkowski, I ain't got the words."

I patted his hand. "Don't worry, Armand. I got a favor you can do for me."

My therapist told me that I play the slut because of a lack of self-esteem. I thought I played the slut because it makes me feel dirty and the sex is hotter when it's dirty. I still like to play the slut, but I'm more particular about who I play with these days. It takes more than a big man with hair on his chest and beer on his breath to bring me to my knees.

Most men don't ask, but the occasional lover wants to know why I have a tattoo on my left breast, just above the nipple, of a heart that's been torn in two. If they ask, I tell them it's to remind me that, in this business, things are never what they seem. In this business, it's wheels within wheels, mysteries without a clue.

Sometimes, on cold winter nights, I awaken alone to the sound of the bitter north wind. I sit up and take out my breast. By the light of the pale moon reflected off the lake, I study the ink on my flesh and remember what it was like to hold a killer in my arms.

ALICIA NIGHT ORCHID

A lawyer by training, a chef by trade, and a writer by necessity, Alicia Night Orchid lives in New Orleans and Manhattan Beach, California, where the sand is cool and the people are hot. Alicia's stories have appeared online and in print at Clean Sheets, Ruthie's Club, Sliptongue, Oysters and Chocolate, For the Girls, the Erotica Readers and Writers' Association, and Jacques Magazine.

You can also read her stories in the anthologies *Oysters and Chocolate: Erotica of Every Flavor, Swing: Adventures in Swinging by Today's Top Erotica Writers,* and *Coming Together: Against the Odds."* Check out Alicia's website at
www.anightorchid.com

Bittersweet

2010 EPIC Award Finalist.

Stories of tainted, bittersweet erotica, written in a literary, engaging, style by debut author Amber Hipple.

Not all love stories have happy endings. Be moved by the cycle of wanting to be wanted and the pain of wanting too much.

$7.99 US, £4.99 UK, $5.99 eBook download

Got Men?

Author G.A. Hauser takes the reality show phenomenon a step further in her original m/m erotica story, *Got Men?*

The set up for the big 'reveal' on the reality show Got Men? is more than just a simple decision. It's about taking a risk. The producers of the show want the subjects to take that chance, because to them, ratings mean everything.

$15.99 US, £8.99 UK, $5.99 eBook download

Future Perfect – A Collection of Fantastic Erotica

Speculative erotica at its best from author Helen E. H. Madden, from the adventures of a sexually obsessive superhero to the best orgasm you'll ever have – at the end of the universe.

Helen takes erotica to a whole new level in this astounding collection!

$11.99 US, £8.99 UK, $5.99 eBook download

Scouts

An overpopulated space station threatens to separate two young loves. At any moment, Challers Dizen could find himself conscripted by the Fleet and forced to become one of their lethal, over-muscled Marines, while Valka Parl could be taken away by the gluttonous Merchants. Their only hope to stay together is to join the mysterious Scouts.

$12.99 US, £9.99 UK, $5.99 eBook download

Messalina: Devourer of Men

Eva Cavell is a woman with an embarrassing secret...

A tenure-track instructor at a private Denver college, despite desperate attempts to maintain control, Eva's world is spiralling into chaos. As emotional pressures build inside her, an explosion is imminent. Will she ever be able to live her life how she wants and without shame?

$12.99 US, £8.99 UK, $5.99 eBook download

Find our books at www.logical-lust.com, Amazon, Barnes & Noble, and all good online retailers!

Logical-Lust Publications

"Taking the Reader Down a Different Path"

www.logical-lust.com

Award-winning titles
and award-winning authors